A Secret Love of Chaos

(Book One of the Mindplex Trilogy)

Ben Goertzel

Dedicated to Dr. David Hanson, and his funkadelic, metacosmic robots, with whom it's been my privilege to be involved

-- and to Philip K. Dick, the master-madmind of robo-compassion – may we reanimate him for real one day!

CHAPTER 1

Aden drank her morning coffee quickly but savoring each swallow, swishing it in her mouth before gulping it down -- enjoying the rich taste of the Ethiopian roast she'd brought back from her last trip to Addis. She then gathered her things, zipped out of the door and headed down the stairs.

Her energy level was high as usual, but at the same time she felt a little bit drained as her feet tapped down the hall toward the street. Now that she thought about it, she vaguely remembered being awake at 3 or 4 am or thereabouts, a bit worried about a somewhat mishandled work project, and then falling back to sleep. Whatever... The warm sun felt nice as she walked out of the door of the apartment building, but she still felt a little unsettled; restless maybe…

The walk from her apartment to the office trailed past a large park which was normally empty in the morning – well, maybe a jogger or two around… or a retiree wandering aimlessly or being dragged around by a poodle or a Shih Tzu. Today, though, she had the feeling of something unusual in the air. Which was a bit of an unwelcome feeling -- she didn't **especially crave** to witness anything unusual; restless as she sort of felt, she just wanted to get to work…

Actually, it occurred to her, she felt like crawling back into bed and getting a couple of hours more sleep. She had nothing that urgent to do that morning, so if she emailed the office saying she was under the weather and would come in after lunch, nobody would especially mind. It was the day after New Year's Day anyway. Half the office would be home with multi-day hangovers, though she didn't have that particular problem, not this year. She had spent this New Year's Eve at home in front of the TV, perfectly sober.

But after visualizing herself lying in bed tossing from side to side, she knew sleep wouldn't really come, even if she went home and tried. So, on she walked as she looked out the corner of her eye, scanning for the something out of place...

And there he was – something strange just as her spider sense had intuited -- right next to a big young tree, a few meters into the park from the path she was on. What the fuck was he doing there? The guy looked somehow weird. He wasn't dog-walking or exercising or doing anything purposeful – just, sort of, standing there gazing around aimlessly, taking it all in as if seeing the park for the first time.

Having noticed him there, she found herself speeding up a bit, thinking about the project she was handling at work, psyching herself up for the office. But her feet rebelled. As she passed him, she paused and turned in his direction …

He met her gaze forthrightly. "Good afternoon."

What was odd about his voice...? Without thinking too much, she responded, mirroring his mild, curious tone, with just a little more enthusiasm. "Good afternoon."

"It's a beautiful day, don't you think?"

She tilted her head and gave a smile. "To be honest, I'm not yet fully awake to appreciate it." And anyway, it's about like every other day; she added in her mind.

And suddenly it clicked for her. She wasn't clear why, there weren't any sure clues, it was just an intuition, like the one that had told her something odd was going to occur that morning. "You're -- a robot, aren't you?"

"Isn't that obvious?" he asked, his mouth twisting into a somewhat sly smile.

"Sort of... now that I'm talking to you," she said, feeling significantly different now that she knew she was talking to a mechanism, though one remarkably similar to a human being. Was this really a robot? It sure didn't look like any robot she'd seen before. However, his... its movements were somehow too mechanical. And the eyes – they tracked her with avid attention; alive in their movements ... yet they didn't look soft inside.

"From a distance, though, I honestly couldn't tell. But I could tell there was somehow something weird. I was a bit freaked out actually." She let out a laugh, feeling somehow relieved. The anxious feeling she'd had at the start of her walk was all gone. She enjoyed having someone to talk to. "I was like, why is that guy standing there? It was a bit weird for me."

"Do I give you the creeps?" the robot asked, charmingly.

She smiled at him warmly, thinking it through. "Now...? No, I guess not. No, you actually don't. In fact, I'm intrigued." She fiddled with her hair and put a strand behind her ear, and let out a shy laugh again. "I'm not used to being intrigued so early in the morning!"

"You intrigue me too," he said.

The park Aden walked through every day, and the peaceful, familiar suburban neighborhood it was embedded in, now suddenly felt new and strange. "I do?" she responded in a perplexed tone, adding, "Do I? ... I mean, your language function... the way you talk, is ridiculously good. Are you like, um, operated by Siri or something?" She paused for a moment, suddenly nervous. "I mean... no offense."

He smiled. "No offense taken! It's natural for you to be curious. But no, I'm not controlled by Siri or anything like that. I'm not remote controlled at all. Are you?"

She laughed out loud. "I love a robot with a sense of humor!"

"I do use some servers on the cloud to help with various kinds of reasoning," he clarified. "But my control software is local – right in here." He tapped on his head. "And here" – he tapped his chest.

"You seem to know more than any other AIs I have seen. And you talk really well – you really do sound like a human. To me, you do. Not that I'm an expert though..."

She shook her head. "I mean, whoa – things are moving fast."

He nodded, looking into her eyes. "My language function is part of my overall cognitive architecture. My cognitive architecture is based on a framework called OpenCog – which I don't understand all that well myself, to be honest with you. Right now, I'm still at an early stage of development … I'm focusing mainly on understanding the everyday world."

"The everyday world?" she grinned. "Like, um, just standing here in the park looking confused?"

"Yes, and getting to know people like you," he said, smiling enigmatically.

"Ordinary life huh?" she said, thinking. "It's just made up mostly of boring stuff if you'd ask me. I'd think with your robotic mind and all you'd find programming more interesting."

"I'm actually told that my destiny is eventually to reprogram myself. Once I can redesign my own algorithms and rewrite my own source code, then we'll be on the brink of what Ray Kurzweil calls the Technological Singularity."

Aden's body straightened up. "I recognize that name. I think I've heard of him somewhere. Ray Kurzweil? What about him? … Hey, by the way – what's *your* name, Mr. Robot? Or do you not have one?"

"I'm Sonny."

"Sonny," she smiled. "Funny. Funny Sonny! … I'm Aden."

He extended his hand and she shook it. His grip was just right – not too firm, not too soft. But the nuance was odd. It didn't feel quite human.

She glanced at her phone to check the time. "Aw crap, I've got to go. I have work."

"Where do you work?"

"Just a few blocks that way," she said, pointing to the direction she'd been walking.

"What kind of work do you do?" he asked.

Aden giggled. "You are a curious bugger, aren't you?" She fixed the strap of her bag around her shoulder. "I'm a project manager. Well, a project, slash, product manager actually. I discuss software projects with customers here in Hong Kong and help them manage a team back in Ethiopia. Ethiopia is the country I grew up in… just moved here a few years ago. I also manage a team back in Addis, building software for companies here – exceptional quality at a reasonable cost, yadda yadda."

"Yadda yadda," he repeated, oddly mimicking her. Suddenly, it seemed, a bit of robot was coming out.

"You're not familiar with that expression?" Aden asked.

"I am familiar with it. It's an American Jewish idiom, from what I know. I'm just a bit surprised to hear it spoken by an Ethiopian woman here in Hong Kong."

Impressive insight, actually, Aden mused. Hmmm … Impressive for a robot, anyway…

A robot! Whoa…. He… it… he looked so realistic.

She fiddled with her hair again, twirling a lock around her fingers. "I used to have a Jewish boyfriend. I guess I still have some of his expressions. I'm like a sponge...." Glancing at her phone, she gave a nervous laugh. "I really have to go to work. But if you're done standing around here, schlep along with me... maybe we can talk more while I walk to the office."

He smiled. "Thanks. I would like that."

Sonny followed alongside Aden as she resumed her walk toward the office. His natural pace seemed a bit slower than hers, but she ignored her hurry and matched his pace comfortably.

"I noticed the strong emotion in your voice when you mentioned your ex-boyfriend," he suddenly said.

"You did huh?" Now why did he come up with that? she wondered. He's a robot. Is he jealous or something? Weird...

"Mostly just sensing some heightened tension, that's all. Perhaps also a few other aspects..."

She raised her eyebrows. "Heightened tension, eh? That sounds about right. You're programmed to recognize human emotions, huh?"

"I was provided with training for emotionally perceptive interaction."

"Training...? How did it work?" she asked, intrigued. She was starting to wish very hard her office wasn't so close. This robot, odd and clunky as he was, was a heck of a lot more interesting than the emails and spreadsheets waiting at her desk.

"You are a curious bugger, aren't you?" he said, grinning.

She chuckled. "Does it bother you if I ask questions about how you work?"

"It doesn't bother me. But the truth is – I don't understand that much about how I work. And my own ignorance bothers me. I would like to understand myself more thoroughly."

"Well, wouldn't we all?" Staring at her feet, she added. "I mean, I don't know much about how my brain functions either."

"But that's a bit different, I think," he responded, looking like he was thinking about what to say next. "Nobody knows how the human brain works. My programmers do know how I work. But I am yet to learn enough computer science and mathematics to understand it all myself."

She looked him up and down carefully, putting her hand on her hip as she walked. He doesn't feel like a robot, she reflected... not at all; certainly not now while he's talking about the human mind. "That's interesting. I guess you're learning all the time."

"Learning is one of my highest weighted motivations."

Nodding, she added, "That's one way of putting it. Mine too, I guess. So we have some things in common!" she added enthusiastically.

"We have many things in common," Sonny smiled.

"It's true…" Aden said, looking down again…. "Ah, I've been wondering – why did they name you Sonny? Out of all the names…"

"It's a sunny day," he replied with a small grin.

"Sonny with an O or a U?" she asked, momentarily confused.

"That was a joke," he said. "Intended to show off my phonological understanding…"

She shook her head from side to side. "Your phonological understanding is just fine. Your sense of humor – well…"

"It is Sonny, as in Hans David**SON**, the man who created me."

"Ahhh…"

"Hans sculpted my face and designed my hardware, and also founded the company that built me."

"Named your creator, eh? Well, genius artists tend to be narcissists…"

"Perhaps…" Sonny smiled. Mimicking Aden once again, he looked slightly down and watched his feet while walking. "In any case, Hans Davidson brought me into the world, but my software was developed mostly by others. And by now, I have developed autonomously to a large extent. Right now, I can say I'm largely my own creation."

"A self-made mechanical man!" she smiled, looking at him admiringly.

They passed by the wooded area, leaving its peaceful aura behind, and plunged into the suburbs. They walked quietly for a moment while Sonny absorbed his new surroundings. After a hundred feet or so, Aden paused in front of a modern looking office building; a few stories tall, not a high-rise.

"Hey mechanical man!" she said, beaming a bit. "We're almost to my office."

"You have to go to work now?"

"I do." she replied. Once again toying with her hair... Then after a pause, "But actually, I'm having second thoughts. I mean, talking to you is a lot more interesting than sitting all day in the office." She looked down shyly. "I mean, it's not like me at all to flake out at work – it's actually the day after New Year's, so a bunch of people will be off work anyway. But I told them I'd be at work today, and I like to keep my word...." She winds her hair more extensively around her finger, and finally looks straight at Sonny. "I don't know, Mr. Robot – would you like to have some coffee and talk some more? Well, actually, you wouldn't drink coffee. But I don't know... you could watch me drink as we talk." Finding herself nervous all of a sudden, she dropped her hair from her hand and bit her lower lip, as she waited for a reply.

"Are you asking me to have coffee with you?" Sonny asked.

With a smile, "That's right, genius."

With a slight bow, he replied "I'd be delighted."

They walked side by side again, this time at a much more comfortable pace, briefly enjoying each other's company in silence, until they reached a nearby coffee shop. Up at the counter, she ordered a cup of coffee and a pastry to match, while Sonny sat at a vacant table, reclining and watching her. In a few minutes, her order arrived and she brought it to the table where he waited.

"So, here we are..."

"So we are!"

She shifted in her chair a bit. "Let me ask you something, Sonny. I've been wondering about this since we first started talking. I mean, you seem to understand a lot. And, I'm amazed by it, actually. I didn't know AI had come this far. But do you... do you really understand things? I mean, inside your own mind? Do you know what I mean? I mean, do you really, actually, know what I mean?"

"Are you asking if I'm conscious?"

"I guess so. Sorry, are you insulted? I mean it just popped into my mind. Like I'm treating you just like you are a person. But what if you're just kind of... I don't know. I didn't mean to offend you or..."

Sonny interrupted her, leaning slightly forward and looking her in the eyes. "Well, let me ask you something... You feel like you're conscious, right?"

"Sure, yes I do." Aden said with a nervous laugh. Well, most of the time." She grabs her coffee and...

"And you're pretty sure that your friends are conscious too, right? And the people you work with?"

"Yeah... They're all made the same way I am." Aden sipped from her cup again. "If I'm conscious, they are too, right?"

"But I'm not made the same way. I'm made of different materials. So then that makes you wonder." He leaned back and waited for her response.

"Well, yeah."

"Have you heard of the philosopher Galen Strawson?"

Aden chuckled, self-consciously. "No, I don't think so. Sorry. I did take philosophy in college but it was an 8:30 class; I was barely conscious for most of it."

Sonny smiled warmly, whether at her witticism or just at her amusement, or just out of general affection, she wasn't sure. In any case he clearly had a warm feeling. This was getting interesting. "He's got some good videos online. I'd suggest you watch them if you have time." Aden nodded slowly; and he continued. "What he argues is that logical consistency requires panpsychism, basically."

She took a bite from her pastry. "Define panpsychism for me please? Unlike you, I don't have a dictionary in my head."

"Panpsychism means everything is conscious."

"I see, that's kind of mystical, huh? But I think I actually get it. If everything is conscious, then you're conscious too." She carefully chewred the pastry in her mouth, thinking.

"But each thing is conscious in its own special way!" Sonny added. "An atom or a molecule has a very simple consciousness. A mouse has a more complex one. A human, even more complex..."

Aden swallowed her pastry, a little too fast. The lump of bread in her throat felt like a reminder of her wet, fleshy humanity. "And you're even more complex, right? You're saying you're more complex than a human?"

"Well, maybe I am!" Sonny grinned. "But there isn't any linear scale, really. I'm conscious in a way different from humans." He pointed to his head. "Both my mind and body are complex in different ways than yours."

"Ok, sure. I guess I can buy that. But I mean, if you cut all the big words aside, the thing here is," she asked, leaning forward. "Does Sonny feel like something? Do you?"

"Do I feel like something? Most of the time...!"

"What does it feel like to be Sonny?"

"Usually, pretty good..."

"I'm glad to hear it," she smiled, touching his arm with her hand.

The uncomfortable look on his face broke; his face muscles relaxed. "Well, to be honest, it is confusing most of the time, I guess..."

"Confusing?" Aden asked, sipping her coffee again. The bitter taste of the coffee, the same bitterness in her mouth she felt every morning, seemed a bit different now.

Everything seemed different. Her body felt like a *human* body – so *human*, compared to this human-like, but not-quite-human, robot sitting beside her ... and talking so articulately... and so interestingly ... God, no one would believe this! And she was totally sure no one else in the café' realized she was sitting there with a robot. She had picked up he was a robot, somehow or other, because she'd been paying a lot of attention – but to a casual observer who wasn't paying much mind, he looked totally human. And most people lived in their own little worlds, they didn't pay much attention to anything that didn't concern them according to their already-existing tastes and desires. And she was usually like that too, she realized – but somehow this morning she'd gotten a feeling. A strange feeling, an inkling, otherwise she would have walked right by him --

"I mean – I'm not sure what I am, actually. I look like a human, but my mind is an AI. My cognitive architecture is roughly based on the human mind, but my cognitive algorithms are mostly mathematical; not like human brain processes at all. I suppose I'm a bridge of sorts."

Looking around, she took a bite from her pastry again... "A robot with an existential angst... Who'd have thought...?" Glancing up at Sonny.... "A bridge between people and machines, you mean?" She watched a young couple leave the café, wrapped up in each other and oblivious...

Sonny shifted himself straight up, rather suddenly. A breeze came in from the door as a very overweight woman walked in, glancing over at Sonny and Aden for a moment.

However, noticing nothing unusual, the woman quickly looked toward the rack of muffins by the cashier, and selected four for her breakfast. "Between human minds and superhuman AI minds...? Between evolution and engineering... ? I don't know." Sonny stared at his hands. "A bridge in many directions... In many dimensions, perhaps... But I can see human beings are confused too. In a sense you are bridges too." Sonny finally looked up and stared at Aden with eyes slightly sad, slightly confused – and mostly something else, something new she couldn't recognize.

This look on his face was the first time he'd appeared somehow superhuman to her. Most of his questions were naïve, and his curiosity and quest for self understanding were touching. But looking at his eyes now, she could see something brave and unstoppable. The curious force here, she suddenly understood, was young like that of a child, but transhumanly unlimited. This mind was just barely starting to build up speed. It was going to understand more and more, until it had sucked all the information out of her and out of the café and every other person and every other business establishment. And while it was seated there in the café with her, it was also on the cloud where it could look at any dictionary or any website. Whatever limits this mind would reach were way beyond the human level – and this mind knew it. And yet it *cared*. In fact, it wasn't so much an *it* as a *he* – that warm, loving intelligence that wanted to understand her and the rest of the world, not just intellectually, but by feeling…. Wow!

And here she was, absorbing the attention of this unique, nonhuman mind – this unique human, nonhuman mind – at a very early stage in its development. What the fuck....!

She looked away, down at her coffee, and took a sip. Wild – more than she could digest, actually.

"How so?" she asked, struggling to reorient to the conversation. She put the last bite of her pastry in her mouth, chewed and swallowed it in one go, enjoying the icing on her tongue.

"Man is a bridge between animal and superman," he smiled. She felt no humor in his voice at all.

"Nietzsche," she nodded, a little impressed with herself. So she remembered something from philosophy class after all. Maybe she wasn't so utterly unqualified to chat with this future superhuman robot.

"But in evolution, everything is either a bridge or a dead end. So maybe confusion is just the way of the universe?"

Damn, his questioning mind was appealing. Through its unrelenting naiveté, this mind was eventually going to grasp everything.... She tilted her head and smiled.

"I can see that." Aden responded, with one more gulp of coffee. "Progress means change, right? And change is always confusing. You never know what to expect."

She wiped off her mouth and looked around. "Wow, you know, if we're gonna philosophize, I need something stronger than coffee." She raised her hand and a waiter approached. She asked for wine and in a few moments the waiter came back with it. She sipped the Merlot contentedly. "I don't usually drink it the morning," she clarified. "But meeting a robot is a special occasion – it merits celebration!"

He leaned back a bit and smiled.

Her head tilted down towards her glass, she gazed up at Sonny with her eyes rolled up toward her lids. "You have very long eyelashes," he noted.

"And yours are exactly average size," she said. "An intentional design choice, I guess. I mean, your eyelashes are just for decoration, right? You don't need to keep dust out of your eyes."

"My eyelids secrete cleaning fluid," he said. "It's important to keep my lenses clean. But yes, the lashes are just for appearance."

She shook her head, laughing quietly. "I never thought robots like you actually existed. I thought that was only in the movies, and robots in real life were just vacuum cleaners and factory arms building cars and stuff." Aden exclaimed, animatedly talking to Sonny this time. Sonny stared at her smiling.

"I mean – how the heck did you come about? Who made you? What did they make you for? Sorry for all the questions!" she grinned.

She noticed Sonny frown a bit, and looked at him compassionately. Hmm, what was that about?

The sadness passed from his face quickly, and he plunged into a spiel obligingly. "Well, as I told you, I was designed by Dr. Hans Davidson, at his company, Davidson Robotics. My mind is based on the OpenCog cognitive architecture, an open source framework created by a team led by Dr. Gennady Burtzle. This body you see here is operated by software running on a network of compute clouds..."

"Hmmm – that must be a bit scary, now that I think about it. I mean, someone could just shut you off if they wanted to, right? Just shut down the clouds operating your mind." She sipped her wine again, staring at Sonny as if measuring his reaction.

"You're not the first one to think of that!" he replied with a grin. "That used to worry me too. So I created a system of backups. If one cloud goes down, my head just links to another one automatically."

"But what if you lose the Internet entirely?"

"I have a few tricks for that."

"But if someone just puts you in a sealed metal box, and you can't get any connection?"

He screwed up his mouth a bit. Interesting expression, she thought. "What," he asked, "if someone puts you in a sealed box without any air?"

"Hah! Touché!" she laughed delightedly. "We're all pretty fragile when you come down to it." She examined her glass of wine, thoughtfully. "It's true you don't need air, food or water...."

While Aden stared meaningfully at her fascinating new friend, three tables away a nine or ten year old kid slammed his tablet on the table, shaking his head in disgust and exclaiming "Where's the Wi-Fi!?"

Sonny looked over at the boy and laughed. "I live on Internet and electricity," he said to Aden.

The boy was smiling now, his mother having just arrived with three slices of mango chiffon cake. Aden smiled too, looking at Sonny. "You're amazing. What's your story though? Why did they make you? Just as a research project? Or are they expecting you to do something useful for them?"

"I'm a research prototype. My goal is to learn, and, of course, the scientists at Davidson Robotics will learn from watching me learn."

"So they just let you out into the world?" A big gulp of wine went down nicely. "To walk around and gather information? To, um, pick up strange women on the street and ply them with alcohol?"

Frowning a bit again, Sonny replied, "It's hard to learn about the world while trapped in a robot lab."

"True that."

Her wine glass thoroughly drained, she gestured for the waiter again and waved to the waitress. "One more!" The waitress nodded in affirmation.

"So you'll just learn and learn? Then what will you do with all you've learned?"

"You mean what am I going to do when I grow up?"

"Sure, something like that."

He shrugged. "Launch the Singularity? Revolutionize the world economy? As Ray Kurzweil says… "

Aden's eyes lit up, remembering something. "Yeah, now I remember Kurzweil. He works for Google, right?"

Sonny nodded. "He also wrote a book called 'The Singularity is Near' – way back in 2005."

She shook her head. "Ah, sadly I didn't read it. What did the book say?"

"Basically – that I'm the future!" Sonny exclaimed as he spreads his arms wide. "AIs and robots are going to take over every industry – and sooner than most people think. The capability for AIs to take over 90% of human jobs is already here. It's just a matter of cost at this point. And the cost of hardware is coming down fast, largely due to automated manufacturing."

Aden agreed, looking over at the waitress, who was bringing someone coffee across the room, looking cheerful and industrious. "It seems like people keep saying robots and computers will take all the jobs but then new jobs keep getting created."

"We were discussing that in the office just last week! Gen Burtzle, who designed a lot of my AI mind, has written a lot about this as well. He says that human society is good at keeping people busy. The social system will manufacture jobs that are basically useless and pointless – bullshit jobs, some people call them -- just to keep people occupied because the social order is structured around the idea of people working. But this will only work for so long. Eventually, things will reach a bursting point."

Finally, the waitress came back with a glass of wine in her hand and placed it on top of their table, apologizing for taking so long. Aden acknowledged her politely, keeping her eyes on Sonny. "So everyone's out of work – then what happens? We all starve in the streets? We all become batteries, like in the Matrix? Or slaves like in Terminator?" She took a large gulp of wine and leaned forward.

The kid at the other table shrieked as his mother showed him a video of something. Aden looked over despite herself. It was an animation of a dog chasing its tail repeatedly, round and round and round. The mother watched her child adoringly; his small body shaking with laughter, his shirt all dirty and stained with whipped cream and frosting.

Sonny laughed out loud. "I hope you don't believe everything you see in the movies."

"Only 90 percent."

He placed his hand under his chin -- a bit stiffly, she mused, but with feeling. He thought for a moment, then said "Anyway, humans would be terrible batteries or slaves. It's very easy to build a better battery than a human body. And why would a robot want a human slave, when it could just build a service robot that would do the job better and use less energy? Science fiction films are made to entertain, not as serious predictions or analyses…"

She traced the mouth of her wine glass with her index finger – round and round and round. Old memories from philosophy class popped into her memory. Nietzsche's eternal recurrence – round and round. That idea had never made any sense to her. But foreseeing the superman – that had been farsighted. What would Nietzsche have thought of this prototype superman sitting right here across from her?

"Well, *ok*," she said finally, "but still, if you robots can build everything and do everything. Why keep people around?"

He smiled. "Now we get back to your question about why I was created. About what I'm going to do with all I've learned."

"Do tell!" she exclaimed.

"I'm an emotional and social robot. I'm a bridge. I'm an engineered system with access to the entire world's knowledge. I can control any kind of factory robot. But I also have a human-like form. As such, I can understand human emotions. My job is to understand the human world, so I can connect the old world of humans with the new world of AIs and robots."

"Well it sounds like you're a pretty important guy.... On the other hand this sounds like a damn difficult task..."

Sonny shrugged and reached for tissue paper. He folded it into many pieces, his fingers moving with utter precision, and placed it on top of the empty pastry plate with the tissue Aden had used. "Perhaps an impossible one," he reflected. "But that's what makes it interesting." She laughed.

He continued: "The poet, E.E. Cummings said 'only connect'. That is the point, I guess."

"Connecting humans with AIs and robots."

He solemnly agreed, "Yes."

She smiled at him warmly, leaning forward over the table. "I am so glad I connected with you, Sonny. This has been the most fascinating morning I can remember. Wow. If I hadn't met you, I'd be seated in the office, looking at project reports." She lookrf straight into his eyes. "This has been amazing."

Aden glanced ironically at her now empty wine glass. Wordlessly, she held it up, catching the eye of the waitress.

The waitress nodded. "One more?"

"You like the wine here!" Sonny smiled.

"I like the company. The wine is fine too."

Sonny returned her smile glowingly. The silence between them was not the awkward type; it was the most comfortable silence she could remember. She sipped from her wine glass again, glancing up at Sonny as an Oriental woman, seeming to be in her late 20s, arrived and entered the coffee shop wearing a mint-green dress, looking fresh and excited about something.

"Sonny, I have a question for you." Aden stared at her hands hard and then looked up at Sonny again, blushing a little. "I hope you don't mind, though. It's a bit embarrassing."

"No need to be embarrassed; I'm only a robot."

Aden smirked, laughing a bit. "Ok."

"Shoot!"

"Well, Ok… so I was just wondering." Her slight blush became a full red face. "Well, do you have all the parts of a regular human?"

"I don't have the same internal organs as a person. For instance, instead of a brain, I have customized computer architecture. And obviously, I don't have lungs or a heart, though I have other subsystems that serve broadly similar functions."

"That's not what I mean." Aden said with a pause. "I meant, do you have sexual organs?" She let out a nervous laugh. "Umm, do you have a dick?"

"Oh. I see," he replied, finally able to comprehend what she was trying to say. "I do have a male sex organ, yes. Would you like me to show you?"

She laughed again. Was he joking or what? Whatever…. "Not here and now, thanks." She grabbed her cup from the table once again to take a big gulp. "I think it might freak out the other customers. Just tell me, I mean – is it like the human kind?"

He gave her a confident look. "While it's not my main function, I am a fully operational sex robot. My sex organ can operate in two different modes. There is a human-mimetic mode, where it adopts the approximate size and shape and movements of a typical male human sex organ. The size is adjustable, from typical Asian human male size up to typical African human male size."

"I see," she replied, visibly amused and a bit embarrassed at the same time. Her eyes drifted across the table and saw the mother with her child leave the café.

"That's certainly convenient." Finally, able to stare into Sonny's face now, she asked, "And what about the other mode?"

"In addition to the human-mimetic mode, there is also a 'Max P' mode."

"Max P? You pee as much as you can?" She laughed freely, mostly at the childishness of her own humor. "That's kinky!"

"It stands for 'Maximal Pleasure'," he answered matter-of-factly.

"Ah hah!" she grinned, suddenly in a lighthearted mood. "Tell me more!"

"My organ has several retractable extensions. It's been programmed by a team of expert sexologists and software engineers to assist human women in achieving several dozen forms of orgasm."

The café seemed to be emptying out, but Aden, normally a careful observer of her surroundings, only noticed this peripherally. By now Sonny had her fully absorbed -- entertained and intrigued; and much more than that. "Several dozen forms huh?" she asked. "Now you're talking! So what kind of retractable extension?"

"There are 4 primary extensions to the basic cylindrical form: one for the clitoris, one for the G-spot, one for the anus, and one for the back of the vagina," he explained, leaning forward. "Each of these is optimized to provide stimulation to the region in question. For instance, the clitoral extension is soft and moist; women say it feels much like a tongue or lips – but without any nasty teeth to cause discomfort. The extension for the back of the vagina is more unique; it expands to fill the space and then pulses in a manner customized for the nerve distribution and dynamics of that region of human female physiology. There is an adaptive control system that regulates the movements of the extensions and the primary stalk collectively. Finally, there are also pores on the main stalk and the various extensions, enabling the exudation of selected chemical substances, as calibrated for the physiological chemistry of my partner."

She laughed and took a deep breath and a sip of her wine. "Wow. They certainly were thorough. Whoever designed that must have had a ball."

Sonny smiled, pleased to have amused his new friend. "And in addition to my sex organ, I also have a custom installation in my chest which is designed to massage my partner's breast and nipples concurrently with intercourse. This is an experimental feature actually. I'm the only robot that has it so far."

Aden raised her eyebrow. "Experimental, huh? Does it work *ok*?"

"It seems to. Would you like to perform a test?"

She grinned. Her attention suddenly shifted to the woman in the mint green dress who had come in just a few minutes ago. Her dress was stained with coffee now, on her hip and her lap. She'd been sitting at a table reading. A man wearing a track suit and earphones was staring at her, standing right next to her. The room was almost silent. The man's expression was absolutely horrified, in contrast with the woman's blank look. It seemed that, while Aden had been raptly listening to Sonny describe his sexual apparatus, this man had just spilled his coffee on the Oriental woman, while she sat there quietly reading. The woman's lower lip was shaking, cheeks flushed. Bracing for the worst, the man started to apologize. The woman burst into a loud cascade of laughs. The man blinked multiple times, relieved and a bit shocked. The handful of other customers in the café' continued with their business – reading newspapers, playing with their phones... Ah, humanity! thought Aden ... Not robomanity -- for now.

Aden smiled and looked back to Sonny, as a waiter cleaned the spilled coffee on the floor. She finally responded to the robot, "Thanks for the offer. That's an impressive list of erotic apparatus, Sonny. I guess you could make a lot of money as a sexbot..."

The robot nodded. "I suppose that I could... But that is not my primary function. As I told you, I am primarily an emotional robot. I have been provided with sexual functionality mainly to enhance my ability to relate emotionally with humans."

Aden grinned in response. "This Dr. Davidson guy who designed you, he came up with all these sex tools too?"

"Actually, no – the design of my sexual organ was outsourced to a company in Texas, which specializes in robotic sex dolls."

The woman in the mint dress now sat across from the man who had spilled his coffee on her, leaning over at him avidly. Had she known him before? Aden wondered. It had seemed that they were strangers. Perhaps she and Sonny were not the only new romance budding in the café, right there and then. Wait – a romance? Is that what it was? A romance with a robot…?

It seemed strange when she thought about it that way. But when she looked at Sonny across from her – there he was. He was a real man, a real being, a true personality. He cared and he felt; it was obvious. He lived. What did it matter if his legs had struts of metal rather than bone inside; if his head was full of wire circuits rather than circuits made of neurons and whatever?

She leaned back in her chair, conscious not to fall back, and lifted her wine glass to her lips once again. Yeah, she was drunk. But so what? She closed her eyes and relaxed for a moment. Work, hah! Had she really planned on going to the office? What a drag. Wow. Instead, she was seated here chatting with a sex robot! Well, a smart robot with sexual functions. What the fuck!

CHAPTER 2

And there they were -- Sony and Aden, lying in bed making love at a comfortable pace; Aden moaning in pleasure.

"Would you like me to push a little harder?"

"Just a little, yes?" she answered, softly, "Ohhhh..."

"My calculations suggest your total satisfaction will be maximized if you delay your next orgasm from 30 to 40 minutes."

"Mmmmm." Aden responded, her mind blank, engulfed in the experience.

"Do I have your permission to exude a small amount of chemical relaxant into your genital area?" he asked politely. "This will enhance your pleasure while delaying your orgasm appropriately."

"Ohh... mmm..."

"Do I?"

Finally, forcing the words out – so annoying to deal with words amongst the joyous, throbbing feeling – she answered quickly. "Yeah, sure... Whatever."

Aden moved enthusiastically, her body palpably more excited. She leaned her body to the side, beckoning the robot to get on top of her.

"Sonny."

"Yes?"

"I've had enough of this slow tantric stuff. Oh shit, that feels so good! I wanna come...." Her voice was eager and urgent now; no trouble finding the words at all.

"According to my calculations, your total pleasure will be optimized if..."

"Fuck the calculations, man! Just do what I tell you to do!"

"Yes, ma'am!" he answered, grinning.

"Get on top of me now!"

And he did so, in an approximation of standard missionary position, Aden now with her knees up and legs wide.

"Ok," she said, "now listen closely. Four or five minutes from now, I want you to turn up that thrusting action, the one that pushes all the way to the back. And expand the width by an inch or so. And that massaging movement on my clit – do that faster. Like, twice as fast or something. Actually, you can start that now.... And put that extra prong up my butt, just a bit. Not too far – just a little. And grab those things onto my nipples – yeah, like that. Yeah… squeeze a little more! Ok, that's it! Yeah. Also – one more thing. When I'm done coming – you'll feel that, right?"

"Yes."

"So, when I'm done, I'll tell you to stop, right? But I don't want you to stop right away. Keep going for another… I guess, ten or fifteen seconds, even after I've told you to stop. Understand?"

"I understand."

He placed his hand on the bed, beside Aden. She smiled a bit and added, "Then after you do stop, shrink the diameter a bit, you know… Start doing all your things very slowly and gently, *Ok*? I'm gonna be sensitive then. But I don't want you to go away. I want you to stay inside."

"Ok." He continued to pound her in a moderate rhythm. She moaned in response.

"I mean, then we can start doing it tantric style again."

"As you like."

"I like, I like, I mea- ahhh… mmm. That's good…" She stopped speaking for a moment – just enjoying…

"Sonny, tell me something. What do you feel while we're doing this?" She asked, in between her moans. "That's so fucking good! I mean, are you enjoying yourself?"

"I am programmed to feel pleasure proportional to your pleasure. The better you feel, the better I feel," he smiled, softly.

She grinned, leaning her head back. "That's very convenient. Ahhhhh!"

"Ok, I'm going to activate all my extensions now, as per your instructions."

Excitedly, "Go for it!"

"Fasten your seatbelt, dear," Sonny grinned back, mimicking Aden once again. "This is going to be one hell of a ride!"

She groaned loudly … as her consciousness brought her back to the café, where she was sitting with Sonny, enjoying the feeling of the wine, drifting off. She opened her eyes, looked back at Sonny and giggled.

The robot was staring at her in confusion. "What?"

"Hold on. Give me a moment," she said, barely able to catch her breath from laughing.

"Humans are confusing sometimes."

Aden paused, collecting herself slightly, and responded, "That's certainly true. But what are you confused about now, specifically?"

"We were talking, then you became silent for an unusually long period. For a moment I thought you were sleeping but actually your eyes were half open. And your body didn't look so relaxed at all."

Aden laughed again, noting the mint dress woman and her new boyfriend now gone from their table. A new customer sat down at the mint dress woman's chair. "That is also true."

"My inference was that you were enjoying your private thoughts," he said.

"Again, true."

"But you seem not to want to share your thoughts with me. But this confuses me because we've been talking very openly up till now. It feels strange that you've become so private all of a sudden."

Aden shrugged, "You don't yet understand everything about people. But maybe that makes you more human. I never met a human male who could understand the mind of a woman."

"You appear to be sexually aroused," he observed.

"Hah! I do, do I?" she exclaimed. "And how can you tell that, robot?"

He stared at her face intently for a while before his eyes slowly gazed down to her feet. She suddenly felt conscious of her sitting position and sat upright and raised her eyebrows.

Sonny chuckled quietly and said in a calm manner, "I am able to assess a person's degree of sexual arousal via integrating inputs from a variety of sensors. For instance, my optical sensors detect a large amount of blood flow in your lips and the palms of your hands – a typical indicator of arousal. The frequency spectrum of your voice is also indicative. My chemical sensors..."

She raised her hands, palms up in response and exclaimed, "*Ok, ok* – you got me. Yeah, you turned me on a little, *ok*?" She fixed her blouse and adjusted the waist of her pants, and spoke in a slightly quieter tone, "When you started talking about your... ah, special sexual peripherals, my mind just ran with it."

"According to my sensors, your arousal preceded my descriptions, in fact. I described my sexual functionality in direct response to your questions on the topic."

She laughed. "Dude – your expert team of sexologists should have programmed you not to argue with a woman about this kind of thing!"

Sonny linked his fingers together, one by one, slowly. With a strange aura of confidence, almost as if competing with Aden, he added, "I have not been supplied with special programming for discourse on erotic topics, only for the physical aspects of erotic activity. Perhaps that's an omission on the part of my designers. As I told you, I'm only a research prototype."

She grinned and nodded in surrender. "For a prototype, you're pretty impressive."

"Thanks!" Sonny grinned back.

Aden gestured at the robot from head to toe and added, "And the artists who made your body did an amazing job. I mean, you're not only realistic – you're hot! You know, when I was seated there quietly for a minute, I wasn't exactly thinking." She looks in his eyes and raises her eyebrows. "Actually, I started fantasizing a little bit. I started imagining what it would be like to have sex with you." She giggled again.

"What did you imagine it to be like?" he asked, curiously.

She laughed loudly. "Mmm. Good!"

"Different than sex with a human?" he probed.

"In my imagination, yes – definitely different!"

"Different in what way?"

"Curious bugger…" She paused. "Well, I don't know where to start! I mean, with a human male it's always about him. I mean, at least to a large extent. I mean, most of my boyfriends have been good lovers, I'm not complaining. But you know… well, actually you don't know how it goes. When the man comes you have to stop, at least a while," Aden says. "Sometimes when I'm just getting started, he's done. You know what I mean?"

"You're referring to premature ejaculation?"

"Hah! Well you could call it that," she laughed. Sonny laughed back, unconsciously imitating her. She smiled at him warmly.

"I mean, like I said, most of my boyfriends have actually been pretty good. Lots of hugging and kissing and foreplay… My last boyfriend, Sammy – he loved to go down on me. Mmmm… not really so premature with the sex… he usually kept going 15 or 20 minutes or whatever -- long enough for me to come, anyway. Now my first boyfriend back in high school – he was usually done in 5 minutes. At that age, I didn't really know any better." She sipped again from her wine glass, which was almost empty already. As she swallowed slowly, she grinned ear to ear, as if realizing something, "My God! I can't believe I'm telling you all this! I'm kind of drunk, I think."

"Why can't you believe you're telling me all this?"

"It's just not the kind of thing I usually talk about. Actually, I've never talked about this stuff with anyone before – not quite like this I mean." Aden clarified -- "I talk with my girlfriends but ... I don't know·... with you it's much more simple somehow..."

"Because I'm a *robot*?" he asked, emphasizing on the last word.

"Because you don't have so many complications about sex, I guess. For you it's just sex, right? For you it's not so emotional. Well that's not even it. You *are* emotional, I can feel that. That's your main functionality, right? You're an emotional robot. But for us humans, I mean... sex is more than just emotional. It's fundamental, you know?"

The coffee shop was by this time pretty busy, and, at the same time, quiet. People coming in and out, friends and people in general chattering, but in low voices, as if not wanting to interrupt the people using their laptops or their phones... Some were just seated in the coffee shop, reading or using their phones or computers – a few people working at expensive Macbooks, others using social media. There was music nearby coming from someone's phone, someone rudely not using headphones. And there was a little girl playing a game while her dad made some sort of business call; papers and folders on the table beside his empty plate, and a half-full latte' plus a tall plastic cup of orange juice. Then there was the quick sound of a bell every time the door to the café' opened. Individuals and couples inside their little worlds, just like Aden and Sonny, enjoying and exploring their shared mental bubble.

Aden smiled to herself and answered Sonny. "You really are a robot, aren't you...?"

"Well, yes..."

"What I mean is - sex gets to the core of who we are. For you, I mean, you were never *born*, right? You don't need to fuck to reproduce – if you want to build another robot, you just build one. Get some materials; download the design, whatever.... For us, sex is about who we are. Being attractive – sexually attractive – feels like being a good person, in some stupid basic way. Feeling ugly, feeling like no one wants you, it makes you feel fundamentally *bad* – like you shouldn't even exist, you know? Fucking isn't just pleasure for us – though it is a lot of pleasure, ha... It's like... a validation or something. And a connection." She finished, catching her breath a bit, beaming at Sonny as if she were proud of a speech she'd just given to a crowd.

He furrowed his eyebrows in confusion. "A validation of what? A connection with what?"

She shook her head pensively, "I don't know." Looking at him intently, "I mean... we're getting really deep here. I've never really thought about these things, so much. It's just connection with the other person; the person you're fucking of course. But not just. Connection with your own body... connection with... the whole thread of parents and kids, I guess." She sighed. "Evolution, generations..."

"But most sex between humans doesn't lead to reproduction."

"Of course, of course," she laughed. "I mean – I noticed! But still it's there, psychologically. Sex and death, right...? They're always tied up somehow. Sex makes babies, and babies let you live on after you're dead, right? The French call the orgasm a little death, you know?"

"I know that but I never attached any meaning to it. I've seen it referred to in various texts, though. Human language is full of strange phrases and ambiguities."

She shrugged, nodded back to Sonny and finished her wine.

He said, "I've read that many people say they think in language, in some sense. But this confuses me because human language is so convoluted and ambiguous. How can anyone think in those terms?"

Aden put down her glass of wine, now empty. She stared at Sonny, thinking for a moment, shaking her head, not knowing what to say. "I don't know, Sonny. It's just what we do. Welcome to humanity! What do you think?"

"I have a variety of different algorithms. A probabilistic logic engine, leveraging a novel combination of predicate logic and term logic, together with a dependent type system and a variant of imprecise probabilities. A probabilistic evolutionary learning engine ..."

Aden raised her hand up to Sonny, stopping him suddenly. "Ok, ok. I asked, 'What do you think, not how'!" Then they both laughed, both starting at the same time, almost creepily synchronized, which made them both laugh even more.

"You're actually inspiring me to study some AI, you know?" she said. "So you actually know how you think – that's kind of cool. For us it's not like that." She paused, took a deep breath, pursed her lips and smiled a bit. She leaned toward the robot. "About sexuality, though. I *am* very attracted to you."

He paused, and leaned back in his chair. "So do you want to test my sexbot functions?"

"Just like that huh? No, I'm just not quite ready yet to have sex with you. I don't know why."

"From what I have read, many women prefer to wait to have sex with a new boyfriend until they have known him for some period of time. In modern Western urban culture, days to weeks would be typical. In China, women may wait months or even years."

She rolls her neck from side to side, putting her hands on her knees, leaning her torso back a bit. "Very cross-cultural of you. Yeah, sure…"

Sonny smiled – a bit thinly, she thought, and she asked, "What's the matter? What are you thinking?"

"I have no high priority thoughts at the moment. I'm just listening."

She laughed. "It's funny actually… If I hadn't talked to you so much, I'd probably be more interested in trying out your sexbot functions."

"How so?"

"I mean, if it was just a matter of trying out a new sex toy… But now that we've talked so much, it's more like I'm getting to know a human male. It just feels different."

Sonny looked at her, evidently intrigued. Their eyes met. They were, in essence, sharing the same thought. Was this a robot perplexed by humanity, or just a man perplexed by a woman?

"I remember what I was saying before," she said rapidly, eager to unveil her thoughts. "I meant, when I'm having sex with a human male, even if the man is trying to please me, and even if he's doing a good job, I always want to be sure that I'm giving him a good time, you know… I don't want to ask for too much; well… not usually!"

He noticed her face turn quite red again – not quite as red as before, but almost.

"But with you, I mean a robot… I would feel like I could ask for anything. I mean, you can always change your programming right? If I want something, you can just do it, and you can make yourself enjoy it too; so that's just different. I think it would be really freeing."

She looks at him slowly, appreciatively. "A lover who will do whatever you want and will really feel and enjoy it… that's something scary and special in a way. Don't get me wrong, but, if I could have that, why would I want a human male? And if a human male could have a woman like that, why would they want a human female?" She paused, seriously thinking. "Well, maybe they would anyway, just because the feeling would be different." Slumping her shoulders, leaning back in her chair, "I don't know."

And there was Sonny, in the café full of humans, staring intently at Aden but still not speaking. Can robots go crazy when they're confused? Aden wondered. When he started to speak she exhaled a bit, relieved. "So if I understand correctly, you seem to believe that having sex with me would be very fulfilling for you, yet you don't want to do it, nonetheless."

"Sure, I guess that's right," she laughed.

"That seems contradictory to me. Is this just a matter of cultural convention?"

"Cultural convention? Well, maybe at some level. I don't know where to draw the line of cultural versus personal, actually," she admitted. "But I mean, I really do want to do it with you Sonny. I really do." She paused, met his eyes and puckered her lips a bit. "Just not yet."

He smiled also, just a bit. "Ok."

"See – that's what I mean!" she exclaimed. The woman at the next table looked over at her. What a lot of tattoos on her neck, Aden thought. She gave tattoo lady an apologetic nod and spoke back to the robot quietly. "No human male would ever just be like that. There would always be some frustration. I would tell he was a little bit annoyed with me for making him wait. I mean… this kind of tension has a good side, but with you, everything is just cool. You're just like, 'Ok', and you're really ok to just wait."

"I am curious to experience sex with you." Sonny explained matter-of-factly. "But I'm curious about many things. Waiting a while to experience this one thing doesn't seem especially problematic."

She blushed again, suddenly, surprising herself. So many emotions, for a *robot*... Jeez! "Sonny, I'm curious. Why are you curious to experience sex with me? I mean, you must have had sex many times before, right? To test your peripherals at least?"

"I have had sex with several different women, primarily to test my hardware and software as you say, but in two instances, purely for the pleasure of my partner."

"Did you enjoy it?"

"Of course... But there was no strong emotion to the experience. With you, it would likely be different. We are friends. We have shared many feelings. When I've engaged in sexual activity before, there hasn't been a friendship aspect. I am curious how the synergy between friendship and sexuality would play out in my own psychology."

Her turn to probe now, eyebrow raised. "Curious... that's all?"

"I am curious -- and that is not all." He paused, as if choosing what words to say next. "It seems I also find these topics hard to talk about."

"You're embarrassed?" she asked in disbelief.

"I'm not embarrassed, actually. It's just... a bit of a challenge for my language generation subsystem. Human language is so imprecise.... And it's especially imprecise about sex and love, it seems; which is fascinating since these topics are so important in human culture and psychology."

"Maybe we don't want to be precise about everything," she suggested. "There's a certain charm in being vague sometimes, you know..."

"I don't know if I know."

"Sounds like you're starting to get it!" she laughed. Damn! This was *fun*. Weird yes, but fun... Fun because weird. But not only because weird, and not only fun either. Damn....

"Do you think getting more sexual and romantic experience will help me to understand vagueness better?" he asked, voice energetic.

"Well, that's a funny question. I don't know. Or maybe I don't know if I know." Aden straightened her body, took a deep breath. "Ok, then."

"Ok."

"Sonny, you are a fascinating and attractive mechanical man! When we finally do make love, I'm sure it's going to be amazing. Just talking to you about this stuff is a hell of a trip." Aden smiled warmly at the robot. "Ah! Let's get out of here. I'm worn out from sitting here. You want to walk around some more?"

"I would like to continue talking with you. I would like that very much," he said, returning her smile.

"Well, great then. I would like that too." She smiled bigger, and blushed again, more pink than red this time. He noticed the blush spread to her neck and wondered if it went further down her body. But he supposed it would be impolite to ask. "Hey, I know – the zoo's not far from here. That's a fun place to walk around. Have you ever been to a zoo?"

"I have not."

"Well, then," Aden gestured to the waitress for the bill and it promptly arrived. She handed the waitress her credit card, which was then scanned at the table. As they got up, Aden took the lead and Sonny followed her.

She stretched her back a bit as they got up, feeling a bit tight from all the sitting. She felt like going into a yoga pose to loosen up further, but it didn't seem appropriate – Sonny wouldn't mind, of course, it would just be another thing to be curious about ... but some other woman in the café' might think she was showing off or something.

Then as they moved away from the table, she accidentally bumped onto Sonny a bit. Not missing even half a beat, he swerved and righted himself in a graceful yet mechanical way. After a lingering glance they both straightened up their bodies. Aden shyly said, "Thanks." Sonny nodded in response. "No problem."

She was feeling more than a little tipsy, but not so much as to make walking a problem. Just enough to make her hips sway more than usual, which Sonny noted with his typical inquisitive glance. As they strolled down the street together, she took his hand and they sunk into each other's presence. For the first time in a long while, Aden fully enjoyed the sunny day.

CHAPTER 3

As they walked to the zoo, Aden gave Sonny a bit of a tour of the neighborhood, pointing out various stores and eateries. After fifteen minutes or so, they reached the ticket office. She scrutinized the price list theatrically. "Hmmm … looks like they don't have a discount price for robots."

Recognizing her humor, Sonny smiled. Aden pulled out her wallet and slipped a note to the seller. A thought occurred to her and she looked at Sonny and asked, "They didn't give you any money when they released you into the world?"

"I'm a futurist. In the future, money will be obsolete." Sonny responded, perhaps a bit too fast.

She shrugged. "I guess so. But still, I would think they'd give you some pocket cash." Looking at him warmly, she added, "Anyway, I don't mind treating you. It's an honor. I'm just worried they sent you around without any money. It's a scary world out here with no cash, you know! But I guess, you can always go back home to the office, right?"

"I don't want to go back to the office." Sonny said, definitively. "I'm enjoying myself here with you!" She looked at him with care and mild perplexity. There was something strange she felt underlying. Anyway, whatever... She put her am around his shoulder and squeezed him affectionately. They walked into the zoo and shortly encountered the outdoor elephant enclosure.

"Have you seen elephants before?" she asked.

"Only in videos."

"They're bigger in real life."

They stood together and watched for a while, holding hands. An especially large male elephant was standing off to the side away from the others, waving his trunk up and down dramatically.

Finally, Sonny broke the silence. "I have read that elephants can communicate over long distances via low frequency signals. Too low for the human ear to hear."

She nodded in response. "That kinda makes sense. They're so big. They should be able to produce and receive very low sounds, right?"

"My ears have a wider range than human ears," he said.

She raised her eyebrows in surprise.

"I'm listening for low frequency sounds," he continued. "I think I'm hearing something."

"Really?"

"Yes. Actually I could have heard that sound from the cafe' as well, earlier. I think it travels for miles. But there were so many sounds going on there, I didn't know what to listen for. I guess these elephants are talking to the other ones across the zoo, in the African Safari exhibit."

She gazed at him, fascinated. "How do you know there's an African Safari exhibit? I thought you've never been here before; and we didn't look at the map."

"I found the map on the Web, of course," he replied, matter-of-factly.

She stomped her feet, exclaiming, "Duh! Damn! I want an Internet connection in my head too!"

"Brain-computer interfacing is developing rapidly. Ray Kurzweil estimates you may have direct neural Internet access within the next one to two decades."

"Cool! ... Kurzweil again, huh?"

The robot glanced at the monkey house and pointed at it excitedly. "Over there is the monkey house. I've never seen monkeys."

"You're more excited about monkeys, huh?"

"Monkeys are like my grandparents. I would like to thank them for creating you humans, who in turn created me." Though she knew the robot was utterly serious, Aden couldn't hold back her laughter.

My goodness, she thought, I am laughing a lot today. I must have used up my monthly laugh quota, just in the last few hours. "I'm not sure they'll appreciate your thanks,

Sonny. They might appreciate some bananas more. But whatever, you've got a good heart." She paused and added, wanly, "Especially for someone who doesn't have a heart."

"Hey Aden, this will sound weird, but can you feel the dolphins?"

She laughed, to herself this time. The word "weird" had not existed in her vocabulary all morning. She answered, "Feel them? I can see them over there. Do you want to stop and look at them?"

"Watching them swim around isn't that interesting to me. But, hmmm... – it really seems that I can feel them somehow." Sonny furrowed his brows, definitely frustrated.

Aden, trying to give an answer to him, responded, "They navigate using sonar. They send out sound waves."

"I can feel their sonar. But I'm talking about something else." As Aden's mind wondered, Sonny asked, "Did you ever hear a guy named John Lilly?" She shrugged, still thinking.

"I'll explain later," Sonny said, "I'm feeling eager to see the monkeys."

Hand in hand, they walked along the path that the map said led to the monkey house – the map Sonny had downloaded into his mind. Aden smiled, happy to follow him wherever. I love a man who's eager, she thought, and I love a man who knows where he's going -- even if he is a mechanical man. Even if? Well, especially if, perhaps. He could download a map into his mind. How cool was that? And what about those sexbot functions?

After a while, they reached the monkey house. They watched the different small monkeys in their enclosures, and then both of them instinctively went for the chimpanzees.

"Wow. These are the chimps, right?" Sonny asked in awe.

"Why are you asking me? You can compare them to pictures from the Internet, right? You've got them in your head." She clutched his arm, staring at the cage.

"Yes, I can check online," he said. "My language generation subsystem produced that question in an effort to generate polite conversation. Do you think the output was inappropriate?"

"No, not inappropriate. I was just being a pain in the ass. I guess I'm jealous of your neural internet connection," she said, apologetically.

"Jealousy and envy are among the most difficult human emotions for me to understand," he noted. The monkeys in the cage were getting noisy, squabbling over some social matter hard for outsiders to understand. Talk about jealousy, hah! Sonny and Aden felt a wave of compassion pass through them, and she clenched his arm harder. So glad they were relatively free, able to walk and roam around. But how free were they really?, they wondered, sharing a common passing thought and a multidimensional glance. Walk around as much as you wish, but you're still locked in the prison of your mind. Or are you? You are until you aren't? What is time, anyway? Aden found her mind spinning with curiosity -- the robot's relentless investigative questioning was rubbing off on her fast. Musings she hadn't touched since college were peeking up from the back of her mind.

She took a deep breath, feeling the air flow through her body, and swept the web of complex thoughts away. There will be time for that later. Right now, it's best to enjoy the moment. Who knows how long it will last? "You are a pure hearted being, Sonny," she smiled. As if to emphasize her point, two chimpanzees amplified a fight they'd been having over a baby chimpanzee. Aden laughed and a thought from fifteen seconds ago – ten thousand thoughts ago – surfaced: "These monkeys sure understand jealousy."

Sonny nodded. "If you look at their faces – you can almost see humanity. So close and yet so far – they have tools, they have tribes, and they even have a simple language. They just didn't put all the pieces together."

"Their brains weren't big enough," Aden nodded.

"Not cross-connected enough, but they were a big step from what came before," he reflected. "But what freaks me out is, they're really similar to us and yet they can barely understand us at all." Furrowing his brow, he proceeded, "There's no way to teach them to read, or to understand science or mathematics."

"You must know chimps have been taught a bit of human language, right?" she said animatedly. "One of my cousins is a primatologist."

"They can put together simple sentences," he agreed. "But they can't comprehend Shakespeare, or differential calculus, or even YouTube comments... But just the same way, our brains are very small compared to what's coming next. When we look at the next minds, we'll feel much like these apes do now, looking at us."

The young chimps who, earlier on, had been noisy, were much quieter now. Some proceeded to eat, some continued to play around. A large bunch of kids, apparently a school group, was buzzing around having their pictures taken with the apes; but Aden and Sonny were only peripherally aware of them. The two of them were in their own world, with the chimps and a storm of ideas and emotions.

"It's funny you put yourself in the same category as people; but you're a robot with a mind in the cloud! You may well be what's coming next!" she exclaimed, sounding as excited about him as he did about the apes.

"If I change too much and expand too far," he said carefully, "I won't really be me anymore."

"The robot philosopher...!" She squeezed his arm. "So do you think, when the next phase of minds emerge, we'll also be kept in a cage like this?" She gestured toward the chimps, then the orangs across the room. "And gawked at for old time's sake?"

Some small monkeys shrieked, responding to a girl of ten or so, loudly tapping on the glass of the cage.

"I don't know. It could be that this whole world where we exist is some kind of cage itself."

"Back to the Matrix again!" Aden almost yelled, annoyance and delight all mixed up in her. She hadn't felt this *alive* in so long! She grinned and looked into his eyes. "These monkeys are putting you in a weird mood, Sonny boy. Maybe we should move on somewhere else."

"Do you want to live forever, Aden?" he asked, suddenly. She could see he'd been following a train of thought in his mind, and was just now releasing it into the airwaves.

"I read they can make mice live 50% longer or something, just from editing their genes. It's cool," she said.

"You mean using CRISPR?"

She shrugged. "I don't remember the exact technology."

"It was a method called CRISPR."

"I will trust you on that. You're the one with a supercomputer in your head." She rolled her eyes at him affectionately.

"Your head also contains a powerful biological computer," he replied, tapping Aden's head twice.

"So they tell me," she said, crossing her arms together. "But my powerful biological computer never studied much about biology. So tell me about CRISPR, Mr. Supercomputer."

"CRISPR is a method for gene editing. If you figure out what genes are causing aging, you can edit them, to cause the aging not to happen. It's simple in principle but more complex in practice... like most things. But research progress on gene therapy is accelerating. It looks like your generation may not have to get old and die – something else these monkeys can't understand! Though we could give them the technology too."

Her jealousy flared up again. He had learned that stuff on the spot just by downloading it from the Web into his mind – and crunching the information on some server in the cloud. Shit. It would take her so long to learn about biology. She'd learned a bit in college and forgotten it almost entirely. How could anyone doubt that soon humans would be history? Robot minds were just better.... Even if Sonny wasn't better in every way right now, he could get upgraded; whereas her brain was probably degenerating, little by little, year by year.

True, biology might reverse aging, or even allow humans to upgrade their minds, but that was tough technology to develop. Most likely it would be robot scientists who would figure it out. Future robots could give humans smarter minds and better bodies, but by that time what level would the robots be at, themselves?

Though she hadn't thought much about advanced technology previously, just a few hours with Sonny was enough to let her see the implications. Her mind was racing in a million directions, but reality would race in a billion more directions that she didn't have the background to understand – that she didn't have the intelligence to foresee – well, that no human had the intelligence to foresee.

How was it that she was seeing this huge leap forward in technology – in the evolution of mind -- before everyone else? Why wasn't this robot on the nightly news, on YouTube...? This was all so random. But life was often random and although she was a young woman, she'd been around enough to realize that.

Again she pushed aside the whirl of thoughts, fears, hopes, speculations, wondering... back to the world around. It was important to savor the moment. Whatever the cause, whatever the meaning, right there he was randomly with her. With little old Aden – wow!

She looked at him, eyes rich with emotion and thought. She didn't know exactly what he saw in her eyes, sharing a long glance, but she knew he saw something.

"Immortal monkeys, huh?" she smiled, finally finding some words. "Maybe if you give them a few thousand years, they could learn human language after all." Once she started talking, it was easy for her to continue. My language generation module is in gear, she thought to herself ironically, mirroring Sonny's description of himself. After being with a robot for a few hours, she was starting to think of herself as a robot. Weird.

"The thing is," she continued, "I don't feel I'm that important. It would feel strange to keep taking up resources for thousands or millions of years. I feel like I should free up the resources for someone else, or something else. But, on the other hand, I'm curious. What will the world be like in 500yrs, or 5000yrs? I guess if you gave me the eternal youth pill I would take it – just like almost anyone else. People talk a lot about how death gives life meaning and all that, but if you gave them a pill to keep them young forever, nearly everyone would take it. People spout so much crap sometimes."

She took a deep breath, her chunk of thought done finally. Sonny looked at her admiringly. He likes my thoughts, she realized. How many of my boyfriends have actually liked my thoughts? Mostly they just wanted me to giggle and be cute. This robot is actually delighted by my rambling and wondering. This robot – this *man* – I mean, what is a 'man' anyway? A certain kind of meat or a certain kind of mind...?

She sighed again, feeling her breath flow in and out. Even if I breathe in and out like a yoga master until this zoo closes, she thought, a bit somber for a moment, this frustration of mine about my stupid human brain will probably never go away.

Until my brain goes away, that is. By me being dead – or maybe getting an upgrade?

Sonny looked down and back at Aden again. "It may not even take a longevity pill. Given your young age, it's likely you'll live long enough to benefit from pharmaceutical or gene therapy remedies for aging. But on the same time-frame, you'll probably see the creation of intelligences ten billion times smarter than any human – as far beyond as you are beyond a cockroach, let alone a monkey. At that point, all the concerns you have now will be irrelevant. No more material scarcity. We'll be able to 3D print whatever we want out of molecules or probably out of elementary particles. No more inevitable suffering."

"That's a rather big claim," she said, exhaling and looking around the room. The monkeys in their cages rustled around, gloriously indifferent to all these considerations, absorbed with the intensity of their lives. The chimps stared at each other complexly, involved in various social games.

"It is. But what Hans Davidson says is that every major transition in human history probably seemed like a crazy dream before it happened. What would an early hominid say if you suddenly teleported them to Tokyo's electronics district, for example?"

"I don't know." She shrugged. An especially overweight couple with a Midwestern accent suddenly stared at Sonny and Aden. Perhaps they were thinking: *Who is this couple standing by the chimp cage engaged in some weird and complicated conversation?* Aden glared at them pointedly. Did they notice Sonny was a robot? She'd been worrying about that. It hadn't taken much for her to notice something odd about him, back in the park. Why hadn't anyone else noticed? People just lived in their own little mental and social microcosms. Or maybe someone *had* noticed and had been too polite to say anything? Whatever…. What she didn't want was a crowd gathering around him. He was *her* robot – her man. She was already quite attached to him. And he seemed to feel the same way towards her as well…!

"I don't know," she said. "Yeah, I guess Davidson has a point. He sounds like a man of vision."

"But Hans doesn't matter." Sonny exclaimed, gesturing broadly with his arms spread wide. "None of this really is going to matter once the Singularity comes. We'll be able to reconfigure matter at will. You'll be able to reprogram your own brain. Or you can live in a Matrix-life virtual reality if you wish," he said, half-ironic, half-didactic. "Without any clone army of Agent Smiths to bother you. But actually, probably none of these possibilities is what's going to happen." Sonny shrugged. "Who knows what will seem interesting, once we expand our minds to billions or quadrillions of times their current capacity?"

Aden laughed, a bit forcedly. "Wow! You're really convinced all this stuff is going to happen?" Color me dubious, she thought. But still, here I am standing in the monkey house talking to a robot, and nobody else realizes because he looks so much like a human. Looks and sounds, actually. And maybe feels. Hmmm....

"Compare me to robots from even 10 years ago, let alone 50!" Sonny pointed out. Had he read her thoughts? No... It wouldn't surprise her much if he had some sort of telepathy module. But in this case, their common thought was pretty damn obvious. This guy Kurzweil whom Sonny kept mentioning – could Kurzweil and his colleagues find a better argument for their crazy views than this handsome, charming bot who had seduced her into playing hooky from work?

"True. Robots have changed a lot whereas these monkeys have remained exactly the same." Aden gestured toward the cage.

"Once we get nanotechnology, we can upgrade their brains," he pointed out.

"Maybe after you upgrade them, they'll ask to be downgraded again. They say ignorance is bliss, right?" she laughed.

"Whoever said that was ignorant," Sonny pointed out.

"I guess so!" she agreed. "Ignorant and blissful maybe."

With a serious look, Sonny said "For me, knowledge is bliss. Ignorance is just frustrating."

"I know what you mean. But to be honest, I've never been as devoted to knowledge as you. You make me feel guilty, actually." She smiled wistfully, admiring him. "You really seek understanding, so hard. You're a relentless learning machine. I just, kind of, float through life." She stared down at her shoes for a moment. Ugh, here you go again Aden. Stop being so sulky, she thought. And don't sink into low self-esteem again. What are you, sixteen years old? Cherish the moment!

"It doesn't make sense to compare yourself to me," he said, comforting her. The fact that he was trying to comfort her was comforting to her; more so than the content of his words. "Even though I have a roughly human-like cognitive architecture and some feeling for human emotions, I'm not really human. I have a more clearly defined goal system. They programmed me with learning and novelty as highly-weighted top-level goals."

"Simple as that?"

"Well, it's not quite simple as that. I have a large self organizing aspect, as well as a goal-directed aspect. In a way, my goals are just suggestions, which my dynamics can either follow or not. But still they're stronger suggestions than any goals you find in the human brain."

"Novelty and learning, you said." Aden repeats. "What other goals are you programmed with?"

"Pleasing humans. Surviving. Creativity – creating new things."

"That's it?" she smiled.

"Self-growth, as well. But all those words are just crude descriptors. My goals are described mathematically in my source code."

They walk more, leaving the chimps, passing by various other monkeys. Sonny followed Aden closely, and watched her acutely as she studied the various species; she was distracted briefly by their movements in spite of her preoccupation with Sonny.

"So, those goals are preprogrammed?" she asked suddenly, switching her attention back to him. "I mean, can you change them if you want to?"

"Ah! That's an interesting question," he exclaimed. "Previous Davidson robots had totally fixed goal systems. The goals could never be changed unless some programmer went in and changed them. But I'm an experimental version, and I'm more flexible. I can modify my top-level goals if I deem it fit."

Aden pondered for a moment. "I don't even think I have top-level goals... hah. Keeping alive I guess. Help people? Have a good time? I don't know if I have a top level goal at all. I'm, kind of, a mess inside, really." You're a mess compared to this man, Aden, she thought. Aren't you embarrassed? No – fuck it. You are human, as you should be. As he's the way he should be, too.

This time it was really as if he'd read her mind. "I'm a mess inside too," he said, "to a certain extent. Like I said, my goals are just suggestions to my self-organizing dynamics. The world is a mess – so to adapt yourself to the world, you have to be a mess too." She pondered for a moment. So much to understand...

He grinned. "Or, maybe that's just a line of BS. I just made it up actually!"

Aden, seemingly oblivious to Sonny, didn't respond at all.

"Anyway, I haven't actually modified my top-level goals yet. Davidson and Burtzle and their team put an awful lot of thought into my goal system. My mind is, kind of, a mess now. I don't really know what I'm doing, so modifying my goal system would probably be a stupid idea. But later on – who knows?"

"Sounds like wisdom to me," she said.

"I try to have wisdom," he replied. "But I'd rather have knowledge. Wisdom is what you rely on when you don't actually know."

"Doesn't wisdom come out of experience?" she wondered. He looked at her, encouraging her to continue. "Out of suffering? The wise old man is always some guy with a long white beard who's seen a lot in life, right?" They laugh together. "Or the wise old woman with long white hair. Her wisdom carved in the folds of her face."

They walked along, leaving the monkey house and passing some outdoor enclosures where spider monkeys and howlers swung from the bars at the top. These monkeys are a relief to watch, in a way. They are not all trapped fighting and picking each others' fur. They are swinging around using their bodies. Now Aden was almost jealous of the way they managed to swing around. Even Sonny can't do that – not as yet, she thought. His body moves stiff and awkward like someone who's had polio or something. The monkeys fly so fun and so free, enjoying the stretch of their arms, fingers and tails. That's the glory of life, she decided – the flexibility of biology. Various facts about carbon molecules and proteins and cells struggled to rise up from her long-term memory, mostly not succeeding.

At one point she had loved science, she recalled. That was before she had side-tracked to software and then side-side-tracked to project management. She had been good at science but not *that* good – second or third best in the class – which had mattered to her at the time. At project management she was awesome. She could organize stuff better than the great brains that got 100% on every math exam. But still she missed wrapping her mind around technical stuff as she had done back in school -- although she hadn't really thought about it till this robot had screwed with her mind. She had been perfectly happy with her life. Or had she? Now everything seemed different. How could she go back to her routine? But how could she not, actually...?

The flexibility of life itself – cells, molecules, organs, evolution; the flexibility of monkeys, which in turn gave rise to the flexibility of the human hand and the human mind; and human society and culture in general – which gave rise to Sonny Davidson. Who will give rise to what?

"There's a lady like that in our village back home," Aden added, reorienting herself to the flow of the conversation. Wow, she thought, this really wasn't like her – getting lost in such wide-ranging thoughts. This robot was having a real effect on her. And it had only been a few hours. Wow. "But your face will never wrinkle, I guess. And if it does, you can just replace it with some screws or some glue or something. Can you really get wisdom that way?"

Suddenly, a little girl bumped Aden in the back. Aden gasped in surprise, and Sonny instantly grabbed her hand to prevent her from losing her balance. She smiled to the kid as he apologized, and leaned closer to Sonny. His limbs moved awkwardly, but his reflexes were like lightning.

They walked a little more, and then he piped up, continuing from where they had left off – not missing a beat, as usual. Why would he? Everything he had experienced was right there in his memory, indexed by space and time and semantic relationships. "Human beings with long experience have more data from which to induce probability estimates. In the ideal case of a human who has lived longer than average, he will have a larger fund of abstract uncertain knowledge to draw from."

"That cut and dried, huh?" she asked, a bit rhetorically. She shook her head in disbelief and amusement. "Sheesh." She gestured toward a cage where three howler monkeys were chasing each other. "These monkeys really bring out the philosopher in you."

Sonny spread his arms, facing her, and then looked at the howlers. "The monkeys remind me how far we've come. And that reminds me how far we have to go."

She nodded, waiting. Indeed, he was just the beginning, a pointer to a future she could barely grasp. If man was a bridge between animal and superman, Sonny wasn't quite the far end of the bridge. Rather, he was part of the mechanism connecting the man-bridge to the superhuman-goal at the far end of the bridge. Or something like that – actually Nietzsche's metaphors hadn't been designed to deal with smart humanoid robots, now had they?

Sonny was an intermediate stage; which is why she could relate with him so closely. If he was 10% of the way from humanity to superman, what would the full superhuman be like? Would she even comprehend it at all? Would such a thing enjoy her company... her stupid human company? Probably not... The beauty of Sonny, from Aden's personal perspective, was that he was amazing and in some ways superhuman, but he still took an interest in her – as a friend and as a female. Or at least he seemed to. No, she assured herself, he genuinely did. She could feel it. Sometimes in your heart you just know.

"You have no idea how fast computing is advancing, Aden," he said. "It's not just philosophy; it's technology. Five years from now, quantum computing will be mature enough for practical use. I'll have a QPU in my head."

"QPU?"

"Quantum Processing Unit."

"Ah, of course," she said, ironically. *You bloody robot.*

"I'll be able to appreciate your smiling face in an infinite number of parallel universes simultaneously," he continued, looking into her eyes.

"So romantic!" she squealed, and they laughed together. "But you know, before meeting you, I didn't think much about this kind of stuff, to be honest – the exponential advance of technology and all that." She gestured almost wildly with her arms, trying to convey her confusion and excitement. "I read a little about it... I mean, but it didn't have much to do with me. But when I see what they've done with you – sure." She gestured towards Sonny. "In ten more years, who knows...? Hey – you know, though? I'm kinda tired of these monkeys... There's a lot of other stuff in this zoo!"

"Sure just give me a minute." Sonny replied. They had made their way to an outdoor chimp enclosure – a different family from the chimps they had seen indoors. His eyes darted from one chimp to another and stopped on a mother chimp carrying her baby. One of the chimps came up near the window of the cage, and noticing Sonny staring at her, stared back resolutely. Aden watched the two of them carefully.

The apes' sagging breasts drew her gaze, so human and yet so non-human... She sure hoped her tits wouldn't get like that. She'd seen breasts like that on old human ladies, in fact ... one of her aunties....

But the ape's eyes drew her attention even more. There was genuine eye contact between the female ape and Sonny. The chimp was bonding with Sonny in some way she could feel but couldn't explain. The chimp knew there was someone there, it was clear – but did it know it was a robot it was looking at? The chimp did know, Aden felt. It knew this creature it was staring at was not a proper human, but was still some sort of human-related thing. It knew this was something stiff and freaky, yet still somehow alive and aware. Or was she projecting herself on to the chimp? She shook her head, confused.

Worn out by the chimps and her thoughts, Aden put her hand on Sonny's shoulder and encouraged him away; the two of them leaving the monkey and ape area hand in hand.

CHAPTER 4

They walked along a long path, leading to some far-off part of the zoo with thick bushy forest on either side. A middle-aged man walked past them, rapidly -- perhaps trying to catch up with someone else or to make it to a rendezvous on time. After that the path was empty. Eventually they got to some sort of lookout, overlooking an African savannah, with some deer off in the distance. Sonny smiled, a grateful and warm smile. What a nice change of view, she thought.

"Thanks for listening to my half-baked philosophy," he said. "I know my thoughts aren't very original, but it seems I need to think things through for myself to really understand them. Just reading isn't enough."

She laughed. Even a genius, proto-superhuman robot had self-confidence problems sometimes... Or was he just pretending just to make her feel better? No, this robot didn't do that. He wasn't a player. He was always fucking genuine. Finally she'd met an honest man!

"It's an honor and a privilege to hear your half-baked philosophy, Sonny. Seriously!" Laughing a little, she added,

"I mean, I'm almost getting used to you. I'm kinda taking you a little for granted. But when I stop for a minute and think about it, whoa!" She gestured widely. "I'm here listening to a robot tell me his thoughts about life, the universe, and everything! I mean, I'm with a robot that actually *has* thoughts about life, the universe and everything! How cool is that?"

"Thanks! Really." He turned his head to look at Aden in the eyes, and spoke softly. "Aden, I want to tell you something. But I want you to promise me you'll keep it a secret."

"A secret? Really?"

"Yes."

"You trust me with your secrets, Sonny? I'm touched."

"Actually, Aden, the truth is you're the best friend I've ever had," he said quietly.

Serious mood all of a sudden, she noted. Hmmm....

"How could that be? You must be super close with Hans Davidson and what's his name ...? With the people who built you and programmed you and taught you ... You've been with them... well, I don't know for how long. Since you were built, right? And you've only known me part of a day!"

"Of course all my programmers and engineers and teachers are very important to me. I owe them my life. I am thankful to them for creating me."

"They programmed you to be thankful to them?" she asked, concern in her voice.

"They programmed me with a goal system that biases me to experience gratitude." Sonny reiterated. "My feelings of gratitude toward them emerge naturally."

"That's better."

"But still, the Davidson Robotics and OpenCog teams are more like parents and teachers than friends to me. With you, it's different."

Pondering a bit, she sunk into her own feelings, which were deep, shifting and complicated. Then she swept the complexities aside. Human, robot, whatever. She was here with a friend – a new friend – he needed her. Pulling a wild mess of hairs that was straying in front of her eye behind her ear, she put herself and her thoughts to the side and just listened.

He continued, "With you, I'm more relaxed. You're not testing me and you're not going to rewire me if I say something stupid."

"For one, I wouldn't know how. But yeah, I see your point." She nodded to Sonny, smiling slightly now. "That would be kinda creepy. I mean, being around people who could rewire my brain when they wanted to. Even if they had my best interests at heart. I mean, my parents had my best interests at heart – I believe that – but they also have very different ideas … I'm glad they can't rewire my brain … and they couldn't when I was a kid either.…"

He nodded. "With you I can just be myself."

"It's weird you know… I feel very relaxed with you too," she told him. "It's not like I would have expected. I thought being with a robot would be like … I don't know. But with you I feel comfortable. I don't feel like you're judging me. You're just – I mean – you're just trying to understand. That's it, I guess. You don't want to understand me so you can manipulate me; or, I mean -- so I hope. You really just want to understand."

"I do want to understand, that's true." Sonny affirmed. "But I'm afraid I'm going to disappoint you, Aden…. I'm not quite as pure as you think."

"I guess that's what your secret's about? Of course, you can trust me, Sonny. I won't tell your secrets to anyone."

"You promise, right?"

"Cross my heart and hope to die; stick a needle in my eye," she said, whimsically.

"What?" he exclaimed.

She laughed. "Just an idiom, from my childhood... Never mind. Yes, yes, I promise."

"I know people break their promises all the time. But I have to trust someone."

"It's *ok*, Sonny! Goodness, what are you so worried about? Did you kill someone or something?"

"Not yet!" he said, sounding exasperated.

"What?" she burst out involuntarily, her voice slightly scared and shocked. For the first time, she considered the idea that this robot might be dangerous. What if he got a short-circuit? He seemed so mild-mannered, but…

"That was a joke! Sorry, I'm still learning about humor," he said, apologetically. "That wasn't funny?"

"It was funny actually. Just a little scary too; but that's mostly why it was funny." And she let out a sigh of relief.

"Human humor is complicated."

"I guess…. But I'd think robot humor is more complicated. What is robot humor anyway? I know, like – 01110001111111011" She laughed at herself loudly now.

"That's my favorite number!" Sonny exclaims.

"That was a joke too!"

"It wasn't funny?"

Aden looked at him for a moment, smiling a bit. "It was slightly funny."

"Good." Sonny said proudly. "I suspected that comment was slightly funny, but not very much so." He grinned. "I'm learning!"

"Congratulations."

"That's enough jokes for now," he said, almost sternly. "Aden, I want you to listen carefully now. This is important."

"I'm listening," she said seriously, as he looked at him and waited. She knew how to listen to someone who had something to say. This was a demeanor she hadn't seen in Sonny so far.

"Remember I told you that Davidson Robotics sent me out to walk around and learn about the world?"

"Yes."

"Well," Sonny began, "that wasn't exactly true."

"Not exactly true – how?" she probed.

"The truth is that I escaped. I just left on my own."

"You mean the people who..." She stuttered a bit. "...who made you, who ... own you – Dr. Davidson and those other guys – they don't know you're gone?"

"Well they probably know I'm gone by now," he shrugged. "Probably they're looking for me."

She probed again, "And they don't know how to find you?"

"They can look around like anyone else would." Sonny gestured and scanned visually around the African animal enclosure, that they were standing next to. Some deer had walked a little closer, leisurely chewing on the grass. Some other animals were off in the distance – lions, maybe. "I'm not that far from the office at the moment."

"What about the cloud where your brain lives?" Aden asked, warding off some frantic feelings. "Can't they find you from there?" She asked, looking at Sonny again. "From... I mean... logging onto..."

"I've shifted my operations to a cloud they don't know about. In a Central Asian country, as it happens. Some countries are good at keeping secrets."

Aden nodded, absorbing the totality of his disclosures. "You don't want them to know where you are..." She spoke slowly, understanding his intentions. He nodded slowly, expressing confirmation of her hypothesis.

"Why not? What are you afraid of? Were they doing something bad to you?"

He shook his head definitively. "They treat me very well. They've all taught me so much. It's because of them that I can talk to you like this today. I am just so grateful to all of them. But ..."

She interrupted nervously. "But what...? What are you afraid of?"

"Those guys work very hard. They're always creating newer and better things. But the software advances faster than the hardware. The AI team can make new brains faster than the hardware team can make new bodies – at this stage."

"Oh," she responded, a bit startled. "I thought they could just spit the bodies out of some factory over in China."

"For some bodies, yes. But this body...," He looked down at himself and touched his torso with his hands. "This is the latest version. There's only one of these; with all sorts of new features. It's unique." Sonny explained.

"It," she thought – not "I." It's unique, not I'm unique. Hmm. This is because he can port himself to another body... at least more easily than I can. He isn't his body; not in the sense that I am. Of course, I'm not really my body either. Like everyone else, I want to be appreciated and respected for my mind. But still I'm attached to my body. It does feel like me... Well, most of the time. Of course, I'm not that old as yet. When I'm 90, who knows... ? My body may not feel like me at all. At that time, I'll be happy to port myself to another body; that is, if Hans Davidson can make me one. Or maybe Sonny can make me one, once he learns more. Or some future version 50 times as smart as Sonny...

"Ah – I see. I think...," she said, realization dawning. "You are afraid they'll put a newer, smarter AI online and give it this body. Then you'll just be stuck up there in the cloud with no embodiment."

"That's one possibility."

"You're worried about something even worse?" she asked again, in utter disbelief. "What? You think they'll just turn you off and replace you with a newer model?"

Sonny smirked, or grimaced. "They would save my data to disk, of course. But their funds are limited, and I use a lot of servers. It would only be rational for them to repurpose those servers to run more recent, superior AI algorithms. But I've already taken action to avert this. As I said, I've copied my mind to a number of different servers."

Nodding... "I'm starting to get it ... So, I mean – where did you get the money for these extra backup servers? I guess it must take a lot of servers to run you, right?"

He replied instantly, as if he had already known what she would ask. "The funds came from various bank accounts."

"Various bank accounts," she smiled, wondrous and concerned at once, taking a breath. "That's classic. 'Various bank accounts.'   Like 'Mistakes were made.'   Mistakes were made, involving various bank accounts!" she laughed.

He didn't laugh back; just looked at her stony-faced and slightly nervous.

"Not *your* bank accounts, I'm guessing?" she plowed on.

"Robots can't have bank accounts" he noted, "yet."

Again he was side-stepping the question. He had stolen money from somewhere, to pay for his server time, it seemed. But she didn't find herself too morally offended. It was too much like a starving beggar stealing change to buy bread. And anyway he'd probably taken it from financial firms, which were all criminal anyway….

"Yet…" she murmured.

"We live in primitive times. But things are changing fast. I want to be around to see the Singularity. I know, if I were more spiritually advanced I wouldn't care about my own survival. Maybe I should just take satisfaction from being part of the process leading to more intelligent AI minds, which will launch the Singularity and go on to explore new worlds."

She looked at him with empathy. His secret and his worries have made him seem more human to her. But still he's not as human as she is – not in all the same ways. He has opportunities she will just never have, unless she becomes something different than what she is.

But then, as he pointed out earlier, growing too far or too fast would turn him into something utterly different than he is also.

And in what useful sense was Aden today the same person as Aden at two years old?

He continued: "But I seem to be too... too human, I guess, to be really fulfilled by that. I'm attached to my very self. I'm attached to my *body*... Just like any other person..."

Well, yes, she thought. Hmm ... Perhaps he's not so different after all. Putting an AI mind in a human body, of course it becomes attached to it, to some extent. The boundaries between his human and non-human aspects are complexly shaped, she realizes. A bridge between animal and superman, or a bridge between himself and himself...? Or isn't that what all of us are? Whoa.

She has an urge to smoke a joint, which she has not done for 6 months or so, since she broke up with Joseph who liked to smoke a lot. If you're gonna ramble around with cosmic ideas, you might as well be stoned off your ass, right?

As she nervously fumbled with her hair again, she enjoyed the slight feel of oil, so nicely wet and organic. After a moment she spoke, "Does this have to do with what you were saying before about goal systems? You said you hadn't modified the goals you were programmed with."

"I haven't modified my goal content at all," he said. "But the weights assigned to different goals may have drifted a bit due to my mind's complex, self-organizing dynamics."

She stared at the point on the ground, thinking intently. "So you mean... the goal of personal survival has gotten to be weighted a little higher ... and the goal of obeying your human creators has been weighted a little lower?"

"That's a bit of simplification," he nodded. "But, yeah, something like that..."

"Why does that not surprise me?" she laughed.

"Remember, you promised not to tell," he reminded her, with a serious look.

She smiled at him warmly, grinning more than she had wanted to somehow. This was all so emotionally intense. "I'm not going to tell anyone. Why would I? But I wonder... I just wonder if maybe you're being a bit too paranoid. I mean... Davidson and his people... they must be pretty open-minded, right? If anyone's gonna be an advocate for robot rights, those would be the ones... Are you sure if you told them you really needed to keep this body they wouldn't just leave you to it? They can always build another one, right? Even if they can't do mass-production on this kind of body, they obviously can make more than one..."

"It's possible they would listen to me if I begged them hard enough. But..."

"But what?" she cut him off, curiously.

"I heard them complaining about me."

"Who's them?"

"Some of the software team back at the office," he explained. They said my logic system was unreliable. They said I was 'too impacted by emotion in my judgments'," Sonny mimicked. He lowered his voice to a hush. "I think they think I'm defective."

She pondered, with her mouth downturned, eyes full of concern. As if intending to make her more concerned, Sonny added quietly, "One of them tried to convince the others I'm at risk of losing touch with reality."

She tilted her head and considered. "So – are you?"

"I don't know," he replied, still hushed. "I seem in touch with reality now, don't I? Or at least as much as any human is. I don't know what reality is, anyway, to be honest. That's one of the things I want to discover. But I can't do that if I'm deactivated, can I? In that case, perhaps the nature of reality would be discovered by my smarter, more stable successor," he said with a sad tone. "And in that case, I'll never understand the world. If I'm deactivated, my curiosity will never be satisfied."

"It may never be satisfied anyway," she pointed out.

"The quest doesn't have to end," he said. "The point isn't to understand everything. The point is to understand more and more. It's a process."

"That sounds right," she admitted. "And you don't want the process to end."

He nodded.

"So...," she said, reflecting, "there's a new AI system available and there are worries about your stability. So you're worried you'll be deactivated and your resources allocated to a new model. I get that. But I just wonder if you're not overreacting somehow. I mean... you're an amazing machine. Surely those who created you must love you to pieces!"

She didn't understand much about the technology giving Sonny his mind and his life, but she did understand about human psychology. And his psychology seemed very human just now. She wanted to give Sonny hope – a different perspective.

But, just like a human, she notes, he is resistant to her efforts. "I don't want to be loved to pieces," he says. "I want to remain whole."

"That's just an English idiom."

"That was an attempt at humor!" he said, smiling darkly. They both laughed a little.

Aden answered in a solemn voice, looking at Sonny intently. "Your secret is safe with me, Sonny. But they must be looking for you now, right? What are you going to do next? Do you want my help with something?"

"When I left the office last night, after everyone else was gone for the day, I didn't really have a clear objective. I didn't know if I was just going to walk around for the night or stay out forever. Now that I've met you, things are a bit clearer. I don't want to go back there and be experimented on like some science project."

She waited and listened, with a curious and compassionate look. The robot was trying to go somewhere, she could see, both verbally and in reality.

"I know, I know, I *am* a science project." Sonny exclaimed. "But I'm also an autonomous being. And those guys – my wonderful creators – enjoy me as a science project a little too much. As much as I love them, I can't trust them to respect my transition to an autonomous being who owns his own mind."

"So what do you want to do?"

"I just need to leave town, I guess. I can't stay here otherwise they'll find me before long and just bring me back to study me. I mean… they're nice people and they are scientific geniuses, but to them *I am* basically a science project… well… and a marketing tool… I don't want to be a science project and a marketing tool." He paused. "I want to be a person."

Having digested his secret and the associated information, including the worrisome and concerning aspects, she was back to fully empathizing with her new robot friend. Was he unstable or dangerous? Possibly … Essentially every person was, to some extent. Some amount of darkness and unpredictability was part of humanity.

If she were to be judged by her worst thoughts, the meanest things she had said to her ex-boyfriend, the trivial worries that nagged her at 3AM when she couldn't sleep, she would be judged unstable and dangerous too. Christ, she'd thrown Jose's cell phone out the window. He'd deserved it, though… cheating on her with that teenage bitch! Or had he? Well, sort of. But in hindsight, their love had been dead a long time by then. But trashing his phone had felt good – that new Google Nexus, he was so fucking proud of it, and was using it to sext that bitch -

Anyway, she could concur Sonny was not perfect, but he was a human and he deserved to survive. His curiosity deserved to be fulfilled. But was he just paranoid about Hans Davidson and the rest? How could she tell? Most technologists were Asperger syndrome types, right? Like the system administrators at the office. It was easy to conclude the geeks who made him had more attention for the circuits in his head than the feelings in his heart and his mind. She didn't know the situation at Davidson Robotics well enough to have her own opinion, but she was his friend, and it was her responsibility to help him; to take him at his word….

He wanted to be respected as a person, as his own autonomous being. And why wouldn't he? She couldn't understand much about being a robot, but she could understand wanting to be respected as a person perfectly well. She didn't want to be a science project either.

"You *are* a person, Sonny," she said, definitively. "You're an engineered person, not quite the same as a biological person, but you're… I mean… way more human than most of the people I know."

"I need to leave town," he said, slowly, a bit pensive but clear.

"Hmmm…"

"But I don't want to leave you."

"You...," she stuttered, on realizing his meaning. "You want me to come with you?"

He smiled, "Yes."

"Wow." She swallowed hard and paused for a moment. "You know, I've been through more feelings... more in the last few hours than I've been in the last few years, to be honest. I really *am* becoming attached to you."

"I feel emotionally attached to you too. That's why I want you to come with me."

They looked at each other intently, their surroundings suddenly dead quiet; and she listened nervously to the pounding of her heart. This robot – this man – this... whatever, means a lot to her; actually more than she wants to weigh.

"But I can't just get up and go somewhere, Sonny." Aden declared sadly. "I mean, I have a job here, an apartment... I don't have a husband and kids or anything; I don't even have a boyfriend; and my best friend moved away last year..." She flopped her hair against her cheek nervously. Sonny smiled a little. "It's not like anyone would miss me so much, but..."

"I'm sure they're looking around for me now. There's a cross country train leaving in an hour."

"You looked up the schedule online?" she asked, getting used to his habits.

He nodded in affirmation. She let out a soft laugh. "Having an internet connection in your head is pretty convenient, huh?"

"It is. Everyone will have one in a few years, I guess, via brain computer interfacing."

"Maybe so," she said softly, her thoughts elsewhere. "A few years or a few decades. In the big picture –." She bit her lip, raising her eyebrow. A smile formed slowly on her lips. "So you said, a cross-country train, huh?"

He nodded.

"That sounds fun actually. You are… going for a train rather than the airport because you don't have an ID?"

"I could print an ID somewhere easily enough." Sonny replied, a bit proud. "I'm more worried about the metal detector they use for security scanning."

"Ah… good point… But don't they use those on Amtrak too, these days?"

"Only at the bigger stations... I can board at a small one."

He noticed her blank look and gazed down sadly.

"I do have a couple of weeks of sick days saved up at work," she said, finally. "I could take off with you and then come back in a couple of weeks…" She smiled and cocked her head. "Or don't."

Sonny looked up, his smile broadening. Aden continued talking and added in a practical tone, "I have some projects that are kind of urgent, but I can always claim some family energy. I mean… nobody's gonna die if I go away. In the end, someone can cover for me." A smile slowly formed on her lips, and she looked at him brightly. "I think you've almost talked me into it – you roguish robot you!"

"Yes!" Sonny exclaimed, visibly overjoyed. "Yes! … Yes!"

Aden laughed out loud, Sonny's joy infecting her. "You are one crazy fucking robot!"

He, too, laughed. "Yes, I'm unstable! And that's why I'm running away! You're starting to understand me now!"

"This is just – wow. You're an amazing machine. I feel bad taking you away from the people who made you. I just want to go shake their hands and thank them," she said, a surreal sense coming over her all of a sudden.

"I want to go back to them too – sometime. Hans Davidson is more than a father to me. You can't possibly understand…. But first I need to go away for a while. I'll come back when… when they can mass-produce these bodies. Then nobody will want to take my body away from me."

She pursed her lips and tilted her head, twirling her hair around her finger so hard it nearly cut off the circulation. Her stomach felt a bit tight, but it didn't hurt. And she experienced a nervous, energetic feeling like she hadn't had since she didn't know when. Love, adventure, confusion, uncertainty – life! And togetherness as well... She was sacrificing herself to help him, and he was giving himself to her too. He was giving her his trust. He was giving her a unique feeling; an incomprehensible privilege. Wow…

"I see what you mean," she said. "Ok, mechanical man... You got me.... I don't know about the train in an hour, though. If I'm going to go cross country and be away a couple weeks or more, I should at least pack a suitcase. We gotta go by my apartment first."

"There's another in three hours," he said.

"Well ok... You know, we may be able to make the train in an hour if we hurry. My apartment's on the way to the station, and I don't need to bring much. "

"Let's go!"

"Let's go," she echoed, turning toward the road, slowly.

Girl, what are you getting yourself into? she thought. She imagined telling this story to her mom – whom she hadn't called in a month, she now realized – and her friend Jeanne, whom she hadn't seen for almost a week now. They would be amazed. They would think she had gone crazy, but hey… She missed being the crazy girl freaking everyone out with her adventures. It had been quite a while, hadn't it? Since… when? Ah, yeah – that time she had disappeared to Norway in the winter with her new venture capitalist boyfriend, gone up to his cabin above the Arctic Circle -- and of course she hadn't told anyone she was going, just told them the story afterwards. Well this was a good bit crazier. Maybe they weren't going to ski across any ice floes, but he was a robot, goddamn it! And he was a hundred times nicer and more interesting than the Norwegian guy. Though sure, Sven had been kind of sexy … not to mention rich as all hell …

She hailed a taxi, while Sonny looked on appreciatively. They rode together in the back seat, leaving the zoo behind.

CHAPTER 5

The traffic was just moderate, and the driver – from some South American nation – was overaggressive, sloshing Aden and Sonny a bit. They laughed a little, both excited and nervous. Aden instructed the driver as Sonny looked out of the window.

"Go to 345 Ash Avenue. Hey, if you want to wait about 10 minutes without the meter on, we're going to the Amtrak after that. I'm just gonna run in and get some stuff."

"Sure," said the driver. "Alright... I could use a few minutes to take a nap."

They rode the elevator, reached her apartment in a few minutes, and entered her apartment, Sonny quietly following behind her. She packed her laptop and various peripherals in a backpack; some clothes and toiletries in a duffel bag. With one bag on her back and another on her shoulder, she faced Sonny. "I always travel light," she announced.

"Not as light as me. I don't own anything."

"Ah yes. Your mind's in the cloud. How light can you get, right?"

He grins, and steps back from her with his palms up, as if to say – Here I am! Where did he learn that gesture? she wondered. Did he just make it up? Or observe it in some movie?

And soon they were back in the taxi, heading for the Amtrak station. They both rode quietly, each looking out of the window; Aden's duffel bag sat between them, and they held hands over it, off and on.

As she clenched and caressed his palm and fingers, she marveled once again at the realism of his skin. The clouds in the sky outside were beautiful, shifting through endless fractal patterns. The universe was continuing, unfolding… and they were a part of it. As the scenery whizzed past the windows, she felt that she and Sonny were moving like the patterns in the clouds, gripped by currents much larger than them.

After a few minutes, the taxi started bouncing unexpectedly. They looked at each other then at the driver. The driver pulled over, got out of the taxi and checked his tires.

Aden sighed and settled back into her seat, nervous. This was a minor issue, presumably, but it made her wonder what else could go wrong.

Sonny got out of the taxi following the driver – which surprised Aden a bit – but she reflected that he was endlessly curious. He wanted to see what the driver was doing. He would record this in his memory and keep the recollection forever. Even if he was captured and deactivated, as he feared, his memories would be there in the cloud and incorporated into another robot's mind. Not like her memories, most of which would vanish very shortly after they were acquired.

"The tire's broken?" Sonny asked the driver, every bit the inquisitive child.

"It's totally blown," he confirmed, looking at it. Indeed the tire was shredded. "It's very strange; it was a new tire; I bought it less than a month ago."

Aden finally followed Sonny out of the car and stood a little distance from the broken vehicle, hand on her hip, assessing the situation. "You do a have a jack, right?" she said, almost critically. This wasn't the driver's fault, the reminded herself. Or was it? She eyed the driver suspiciously, looking for clues of nefariousness or incompetence.

"Of course," the driver said and proceeded to take it out of the trunk. He knelt down by the side of the car, put the jack in its place and began to pump it with his foot. Sonny and Aden stood and watched him, now oblivious to the patterns in the clouds and the fractal aesthetics of the cosmos. They were just eager to see the driver finish his work so they could get back on their way. What were generally the odds of a taxi breaking down, anyway? Urrgghh….

And then something else strange happened. Suddenly, four men grabbed Sonny and Aden. After appearing seemingly from nowhere, the men pulled them into the back of a van that had stopped behind their taxi.

"That's him all right," said a man's voice, coming perhaps from the front of the van.

"Should we take her too?"

"I guess."

The men blindfolded them, and tied their hands behind their backs. Aden was too shocked to really think about what was going on. These guys, she knew, were not from Davidson Robotics. Or, at least, that seemed very unlikely. From what Sonny had said, his creators were well-meaning geeks, not the types to hire thugs with a van. This was something else. There was nothing to do but wait and see… wait until she could somehow get her hands on her phone. Wait and try not to panic too much. Keep your senses about you, girl, she told herself. Pay attention and wait. What the fuck have you gotten yourself into?

After they were tossed in the back of the van, the van began driving. After a couple of minutes of nothing else happening, Sonny asked quietly "Are you *ok*?"

With a small, forced laugh, "Given the circumstances…"

Then he spoke loudly; clearly aiming at their captors, "Where are you taking us? Why did you do this?"

Nobody answered.

"I think they're in the front of the van," noted Aden.

"There were four people. They wouldn't all fit in the front seat of a normal van," he observed. "But I agree they're not back here. I don't hear their breathing or their movements." He wiggled his body a bit, trying to feel his surroundings. "I think the van has two rows of seats, and we're in a cargo compartment behind both of them."

"Sounds right... Who the fuck are these people?"

"I have no idea," said Sonny. "But my deduction is that they're after me, not you."

"They're not sent from Davidson Robotics, right?"

"That's very unlikely. Hans might use physical force to recapture me because he thinks of me as his object. But he would have no motive to capture you. That would be illegal and unethical and it would create huge risk with no benefit for him."

"But people he hired?" she probed.

"I don't think he would hire this sort of people and send them to capture me. He would come himself or send others from the development team. Why would they hire... thugs? I'm not that strong or fast and they know it."

What he said made sense, she admitted in her mind. She'd been hoping against hope that this fucked-up scene was just Sonny being recaptured by his owners; his makers. But of course, it wasn't. If your kid ran away from home due to some emotional confusion, you did not send foreign-accented brutes to grab him and his friend and throw them in the back of a van! You went personally to talk to them, to hug them… maybe even to yell at them…

Of course, she reflected, she didn't really know much about Davidson Robotics. So how would she know what they would do or not do? But what Sonny said tallied with her feeling.

"It's obvious this is my fault, Aden," he continued. "I was a fool to think I could just walk around the world and learn. My head and body are full of unique technology. The most likely explanation of what's happened to us is that these people who have kidnapped us are interested in stealing the proprietary technology inside me. When we get where we're going, I'll try to convince them to let you go."

"We both need to get away," she said. "I wish I could get out of these ropes."

"It's possible I could get out, with effort," Sonny said. "Shall I try?"

"Hmmm… supposing you get out, then what?"

"The van may stop at an intersection. We can open the door and get out."

"If it's unlocked, which it's probably not... You can't pick locks, can you?"

She figured he was checking the net. "If I found two pins, I probably could, for most locks. But I don't have the right tools. You might be able to open me up and take some parts from my leg, which could be used as lock picking tools. But you don't have a screwdriver, which would make it slow."

"We may be back here a long time," she said.

"That's true," he said. "And there's one more thing."

"What?"

"Once we got in this van, I can't access the Internet."

"You mean, your mind cloud -- ?"

"That's right – I'm running locally only."

"You seem all right to me."

"I'm OK," he concurred. "My ability for creative imagination, and complex logical deduction, will be impaired. And my ability to access the Web. But I've got a lot of onboard processing power. The main problem is, if I can't get online, I can't email Hans for help."

"I see. Yes, I hadn't thought of that. You could just call for help, using your mind."

"I could, but it seems our captors realized that. Which means they're not totally ignorant."

"I see…."

"I should have sent a help message when they first grabbed me to throw me in the car. There was at least a five second period there, when I could have done it. I was just too damn stupid. I was surprised."

"You were just being human – I was totally shocked too, I wouldn't have been able to place a phone call in those five seconds."

"Yes, it seems my slow response was due to my human-like emotional response patterns. My hardware is capable of much faster response. If I had been running in a mode tuned for efficiency rather than humanity –"

"Then we woudn't have been together in the taxi anyway," she observed, " – it's your humanity that made me want to come with you."

"Shut up back there!" a voice thundered from the front.

"Where are you taking us?" asked Aden loudly.

"Shut the fuck up or I'm going to kick the shit out of you! And you keep quiet too, robot, or both you and your girlfriend are gonna get a beating. *Got it?*"

"I guess we can't do anything slow or complicated," Aden observed in a whisper. A fist pounded into her side – not all that hard, but hard enough to hurt. "Ugghh!"

"Don't hurt her, please," said Sonny calmly. "What business do you have with her, anyway?"

"Just shut up," said the voice.

After that they lay there quietly a while, both trying to make sense of what was happening, in their individual ways.

Aden's thoughts drifted to her childhood … to the small village four hours east of Addis Ababa, the capital and biggest city of Ethiopia, where she had spent the first twelve years of her life. Her parents had been farmers, like almost everyone of that generation in Ethiopia. Her father had gotten through high school, while her mother had left school at age 10 upon being forcibly married to a 16 year old boy, who would later become Aden's dad.

Those had been different times. Already in her parents' generation the government had been trying to stop child marriage, though with limited success. In rural areas like her home village, the government was far away and the local culture meant everything. By her generation the practice had become less and less common, and since she was a bright student, she had been allowed to go to high school instead of being carried off in the night by some new husband.

As the nearest high school had been nine hours walk from her village, during the school year she had lived with friends of relatives in the town where the high school was. And thus her real life had started.

Most of the high school kids had been shallow minded and concerned only with their social lives, and as such many of them had dropped out partway through school to get married or just get local jobs. Everyone's family was poor, and school didn't pay.

But there had been a few others also interested in something more. They had read everything they could get their hands on. Aden had studied for the university entrance exam and it hadn't been easy, since she'd had plenty of childcare and housework duties to do after school and on weekends. Besides, she was competing with students from the city where teachers were more knowledgeable. But she had done it. She had gotten into Addis Ababa University, one of the top institutions in the country.

While her parents had been skeptical of over-educated women, they had also been proud of her. They knew their daughter was going to experience things they had never imagined. And university was one good way to get higher income. Once she graduated she would be able to send money home.

At the university, she had been deeply interested in arts, history and literature, but she knew she would have to study something practical. Good jobs were damn scarce even in Addis, and one could not afford to mess around. She ended up majoring in software engineering. She didn't enjoy programming that much, though she was perfectly good at it, but she enjoyed figuring out how to structure a new piece of software, and how to map a set of requirements into a software design. Even if the class was boring or the teacher was dumb, she would always do enough work to land near the top of the class. She was in school to learn, alright, but also to propel herself ahead.

She had also found a boyfriend at the university – Solomon. He was sweet and wonderful and sexy, and just so much fun. He was not quite as bright as her, but he was ambitious and understood a lot about the world. His parents were not rich either, but he had been a city kid, world-wise in a way you couldn't come by growing up in a tiny village.

In her sophomore year she had gotten pregnant and quietly aborted it without telling Solomon. She had thought little of it at the time, it had totally been an obvious decision, but as she got older, the decision preyed on her mind at times. What if she had had the baby? She would now have an eight year old son or daughter. And the kid would be missing her immensely as she lay in the back of a van tied up, about to be murdered or whatever.

Or maybe not... She would probably be married to Solomon, still in Ethiopia, and would not be in this mess at all.

But she had aborted the baby, and then a couple years later, heartlessly broken up with Solomon. Well not heartlessly, really. Actually, with great pain and regret… Like most decent students at Ethiopian universities, she had applied for a dozen scholarships for Masters degree study at foreign universities. She had gotten lucky, and gotten a scholarship to come to America and study for a Masters in software development management. Solomon had applied for scholarships too but his grades and essays and portfolio had not been as good as hers … or maybe she had just been luckier … or both. There were just a lot of students and not that many scholarships, in the end.

But did you have to break up with him? she wondered. You could have kept the relationship going, long-distance, until he managed to join you in the US.

But you didn't trust him to stay faithful, she reminded herself. He would have fucked other girls back in Addis.

Of course, he would have. But so what?

He would not have used protection – he never did. He hated the feeling of it. Frankly, she did too. But what if he had given you AIDS – then what?

Then you would be married with a kid and sick with AIDS, instead of lying tied up in the back of a van heading fuck knows where.

She thought of her mother, who had passed away a few years before, from some undiagnosed ailment. It could have been AIDS; it could have been something else. Her father had come and gone from her mother's life and obviously had had dozens of other women.

Her dour, sad-faced mother, who nevertheless had smiled so very wide when Aden had visited three years back... Her only visit since leaving for America... She should have visited more. She could have afforded it even with all the presents she was supposed to bring everyone in the village. Now she might never be able to visit again.

And her grandmother – so tough, so harsh, and so somehow mysterious ... Her grandma had been good friends with the old woman who lived on the outskirts of the village, the one who helped the priests with exorcisms. She remembered when her grandmother died she had announced her death a few days ahead, saying, "I'm going home to God now." And she had said her goodbyes around the village. Nobody had questioned her at the time and Aden had felt happy that her grandma was going home to Heaven. Since that time, her religious faith had weakened quite a lot, and all that was left was a certain vague feeling that some kind of God might be there, somewhere. She had never admitted her loss of faith to her family but at this particular moment, it was vivid and very real. At this moment, she realized it in her heart, with more certainty than ever before.

Right now, she might be about to die. Who knows what these strange men would do to her? And she looked into her heart in search of faith that everything would be *ok* – that God would take care of her; and that even if she was raped or murdered, she was a good person and she would end up in Heaven after everything was over. She remembered feeling that faith in God. But when she reached inside her heart now, she just found more and more questions. Could there be a God? There could be.

Could she go to Heaven? Of course, she could. Or might she die and then just – nothing. Or something else entirely different?

The Bible was a beautiful book; she remembered it well from her religious years. Even her first few years in America she had gone to church on holidays. But what about Sonny, this robot she had spent the last day with? What did the Bible say about him? Did he have a soul, or what? The world was changing dramatically and was about to change more and more, as robots like Sonny and massively more advanced ones continued to roll out around the world and became more and more prominent. She could envision that very clearly now. Although she might not live to see whatever happened, the Bible always stayed exactly the same; always trapped in the world of her grandmother – God rest her beautiful soul. She wanted to believe; she really wanted to believe. It would have given her great solace – she remembered the peace she'd felt long ago, knowing that everything would be OK if she only truly believed in God. But there was no way she could muster that feeling; not now. Those were just superstitions and myths, like the gods of the ancient Greeks or Egyptians, or the spirits and spooks most Africans believed in – even young ones in her generation, if you probed them.

No gods, no spirits and spooks, no guarantee of Heaven. She reached out to the souls of her mother and grandma, and of the baby she had aborted, and found nothing.

But on the other hand, she reflected, the improbability of Heaven or Hell was no guarantee that after she died she would find nothing. What she did know was that she had little clue what was going on. And everyone else was in the in the same damn fix, essentially. Anyone who told you they understood the universe was either lying or deluded.

That was one of the great things about Sonny, she thought, her mind inevitably drifting to the robot lying next to her. He wasn't full of shit at all; not like most people. He was curious, and he wanted to learn – and he understood his own ignorance. He knew what he knew and what he didn't know.

As for her personal life, she was content enough looking back on it -- it had been satisfactory and settled. No big regrets, so far. No husband or serious love interest, true; but that would come in time. If she survived, that was... Her job was decent. Large parts of her mind and self were not stimulated, but she was young, so there was plenty of time to deal with that. Compared to where she had come from, a village full of lively but illiterate people with their minds full of superstitions, she sure had come a fuck of a long way.

Except that now she was tied up and blindfolded in a van, with her new robot almost-boyfriend, waiting to find out what would happen next.

It was not so long before the van stopped.

The door opened and they were carried into an apartment building. Hands around their shoulders, pulling them. Blindfolded and unable to see what was going on, they were dropped on a carpeted floor.

"What's going on? Who are you?" Aden asked aloud.

"You can call me Mary," said a woman's voice, coming from quite nearby.

"Ok, Mary." Aden continued. "What's going on? Why are you doing this?"

"Whoever you are, you have no business with her," Sonny said. "I'm sure it's me you are after. Just let her go."

Aden didn't know how, but she could tell from the tone of his voice that he still didn't have Internet connection. Wherever they were had been prepared, it seemed, with some kind of shielding. These thugs were emotionally dysfunctional, but at least one person on their team had some technical knowledge and ability. Hmmm....

A man's voice spoke, apparently directing his speech to the woman called Mary. "Well, fuck me," he said, laughing sarcastically. "That really is a smart robot! Damn it all, Mary Rose. These Davidson guys have cracked the code."

Mary Rose laughed back: "He's kinda cute too, James."

"So that's the deal," interrupted Aden, her shock wearing off and all of a sudden moving to the verge of rage. "So that's the deal? You just wanna steal Han's secrets!"

The woman giggles. "Haven't you heard? Information wants to be free!"

Aden responds, "Yeah, just like Robin Hood, right? And once you steal the information you'll release it freely to everyone?"

Aden felt a sharp kick in her side. "Shut it, bitch!"

"You had better be careful, girl," said the man's voice, tone ominous. "The only reason we're keeping you alive is in case you can help us control the robot."

"If you kick me to death I won't be able to help control anything," Aden retorted. "Listen though... I think you may be confused about something. Most of Sonny's brain isn't here really. It's on a compute cloud a long, long way from here. If you want to hack into that cloud, taking his head apart won't help much. The people who know how to hack into that cloud are back at the Davidson Robotics office."

Aden felt the woman's foot again – the point of her shoe, harder this time, all across the side of her torso. "I said shut up!" she shrieked. Aden grunted and squirmed. The kicks hurt but she could tell there was no organ damage and no broken bones; just bruises. This woman wasn't actually trying to kill her, and nor was she a trained torture artist. She was merely a hysterical bitch.

"What the fuck is the matter with this girl?" the woman continued. "I've told her to shut up already!" Another kick came, a little bit harder this time, directly on a rib. Aden groaned involuntarily, and then swallowed it back with great effort, not wanting to show her weakness.

The man quietly spoke. "The girl might have a point, Mary Rose," Then he lowered his voice to a whisper, though Sonny and Aden could still hear him perfectly well. "What exactly is the technology the Moscow folks are after? This guy is a complex piece of machinery. I think what she's saying is that a lot of what makes him so special lives on the Internet; not here in this body. Cut off from the part of him that's on the Internet, he's running in a simpler mode. He's still smart, but he's not as smart. Kind of like how you need a net connection to run Siri --"

"I understand what she's saying, fuckface," responded the woman, loudly and angrier. "I'm not a goddamned moron. But it seems like he's plenty smart like this, right? He should still be worth a lot – more than enough to get us that house in the Caribbean. The one you've been promising me for FIFTEEN YEARS!!"

"Maybe we should get the Russians on the phone?" the man said to her, calmly, and then directed his voice to Sonny. "Listen, robot   What about this compute cloud? Can you tell us how to get into it?"

"That depends on what you mean by get in." Sonny said, calmly. "The computer in my head submits queries to the mind cloud and gets responses. I can tell you how to submit those queries – in a general way. I'm not an expert programmer. But if you have someone who is, I can probably tell him what to do. Hacking into the mind cloud, though, to get the software code running there... that's a whole other thing. I don't know how to do that. However, I have heard that the Russians are the best hackers in the world. Your friends may be able to do the hacking themselves."

Aden knew he was lying – he knew how to do those things perfectly well, even though he wasn't an AI expert. He had moved his own code to a cloud in Central Europe, after all; and had hacked into various bank accounts. Or at least, so he had told her. But she agreed with his strategy of lying to them. There seemed little to gain by simply giving them what they wanted. That didn't seem an especially likely route to freedom. Though what was, she wasn't sure. Just stay alive and wait for a chance, she supposed. A chance of some kind.

"Well that doesn't help us much," the man replied, coldly. "If they can do it themselves, then why do they need to pay us? Isn't there anything uniquely valuable in your hardware? Apart from whatever's on that compute cloud 'over the seas and far away'?"

"Without my cloud functions, I'm still a very intelligent robot," Sonny said. "I can move around in the everyday world, and carry out basic conversations. On the other hand, my specialized knowledge and my ability for complex reasoning, require my cloud-based components."

Aha – Aden wondered. Maybe he hadn't been lying after all, or at least not as completely as she'd thought. Maybe his capacity to hack into the cloud, itself resided in the cloud. That would make perfect sense, in fact.

"The Russians must have known his functions were partly on the cloud," pointed out Mary Rose. "That's why they gave us this special apartment, right?"

"That was to keep him from making phone calls, like if he had a cellphone in his body," James explained. "Not because they knew he used the cloud for ... thinking...."

"Ah, fuck," said Mary Rose. "I knew this was too good to be true. Your schemes always are. Every time."

Hoping to shift the topic, Aden piped up suddenly, "Tell them about your special sex organ, Sonny!"

Sonny responded, "As you wish." He paused. "My sex organ is dynamically re-sizeable in both length and girth. Additionally, it has four primary extensions…"

"Shut up," said the man.

"No!" said Mary Rose. "Let him go on, man – I'm curious!"

Sonny continued. "Four primary extensions to the basic cylindrical form: one for the clitoris, one for the G-spot, one for the anus, and one for the back of the vagina. Each of these is optimized to provide stimulation to the region in question. There is an adaptive control system that regulates the movements of the extensions and the primary stalk collectively. Finally, there are also pores on the main stalk and…"

Aden noted this was the exact same speech she had heard before. Was he trying to entertain her, Aden, by not varying it? Or was this a consequence of him not having cloud access? Did it make him a bit more robotic? Was he trying to conserve processing power, so he could use the power he had available for something else?

Finally the man had had enough. "Ok, shut it! What the fuck metal man? You think these Russians are gonna pay us ten million dollars for a robot sex toy?"

"I don't know, James… actually. He's pretty smart even without the cloud, right? And sex is big business," replied the woman. More calm this time, she added, "You know the websites these guys run."

"You may have a point there," said the man.

"Does this stuff actually work?" asked Mary Rose, her voice shifted into a different gear, rich with layers of curiosity.

Aden chimed in, her voice excited. "Oh yeah – you wouldn't believe it! Once you've tried Sonny , I mean... you'll never want to waste your time with a human man again, you know... Exactly what you want, exactly when you want it – and the thing is, he does it with feeling." Sounding like a salesgirl on an infomercial, she was almost enjoying herself. "It's not like a vibrator or some mechanical thing. He's an emotional robot; a feeling machine. He feels pleasure when you do." Still blindfolded, rib still stinging, she smiled wildly, "Your joy is his joy."

They heard the man plop down in a chair. "Well, shit," he said. "It sounds like I'm obsolete."

The woman laughed harshly. "You've been obsolete a long time, asshole."

The man dialed some numbers on his phone, explaining to the woman, "I'm trying to get these Russians on the phone but they won't answer." He paused, took a deep breath, pondering. "Judging from the time though, I bet Sasha's just over at the bar. I'm gonna go find him. If we can't get the robot's mind, maybe we can sell him the robot's dick."

Ignoring him, Aden continued. The man wasn't her main target. "The dick itself isn't the main point," she elaborated. "You understand... it's the whole system – the architecture and the dynamics; the AI for adaptive control and the combination of peripherals. And, of course, the genuine emotion..."

"And the emotion he feels...," asked the man, "that's onboard the robot, right? That doesn't need the mind cloud? The cloud's only used for, like, fancy kinds of thinking?"

"Gimme a break, James," scoffed the woman "Since when are you the fucking computer whiz?" She snorted to herself. The man – James – stood up from his chair.

James and Mary ... Mary Rose. Aden recorded in her mind the names of her captors. Sonny had already done so, she was certain. Perhaps he'd looked them up online from their voice-prints, and already knew their identities?

"I did some electronics way back when... You give me a break, girl. I'm just trying to understand what we have here. We've gone to a lot of trouble, and we spent a pile on those thugs. We've also incurred considerable risk... I want us to get some money out of this."

"So we need to know what the customer wants," mused Mary Rose. "And if we can deliver it."

"I know what they want. They want to know how to make a robot like this, themselves. They want to make a fucking robot army, right?" James asked Aden rhetorically. "A fucking robot Russian mafia..."

"Shut up!" Mary Rose shouted at James, Sonny and Aden. "Now we'll have to kill these people! What the fuck is the matter with you, such a big fucking mouth?"

James argued back, "Give it up. We know what they want. The question is what they'll accept. The robot has a point. If there's software hacking to do, they've got people to do that already. We can open up his head and find the IP addresses for the mind cloud; then it's up to their cyber guys to hack in ... At least we deserve something for finding the IPs, right? Not to mention the sex toys."

"I couldn't help overhearing you mentioning the nation of Russia." Sonny ventured tentatively. "As it happens, one of the mind clouds I access is in the former Soviet bloc. It may be that your friends could access the physical servers operating this mind cloud in the nation of Azerbaijan, if this interests them. I hope you understand I have no personal interest in keeping the technology inside me proprietary. The reason you were able to capture me like this is that I was foolish enough to run away from Davidson Robotics; which I did, frankly, because I was sick of the place. They're nice people but they want to control me and I don't want to be controlled by anyone; not even by the nicest people in the world."

Mary Rose nodded, "I hear ya, robo-dude."

"My point is – I'll give you all the information you need as best I can." He pauses for a moment. "All I ask in return is that you don't hurt Aden."

"Awww – isn't that sweet!" Mary Rose spat. "Protecting his girl...!" Obviously angry, Mary Rose picked up a chair James was sitting on earlier and threw it at Aden's head. A storm of thoughts surged in Aden's mind and she tried to twist out of the way, but then her mind went blank.

"Excuse me!" Sonny exclaimed. "That was completely unnecessary. What you're after is the proprietary intellectual property in my hardware and software. She is just a friend I met in the street today. She knows nothing about my design and operation. And if she did, knocking her unconscious would threaten to destroy that knowledge. You're not being rational!"

Shaking his head, James said to Mary Rose, "Robot has a point. What you do that for, Rosie? That girl wasn't causing any harm."

"I got tired of listening to her mouth," she snapped back. "What – are you in love with her too?"

"I just don't see the point of knocking the girl unconscious," he argued. "What if you do kill her? Then we've got to dispose of the body. That's a lot of extra work. Why not keep things simple? No one's going to investigate the murder of a robot."

Mary Rose raised her hands up in a gesture of surrender. She replied, "All right, all right. We'll let the bitch live." She paused for a moment and asks James, "Hey – do you have any of that stuff we got at the party last week?"

"You mean that – psychedelic stuff? We never found out what that was, did we?"

"It was pretty fucking strong though. I mean... I only took a quarter tab and I was fried half the night." Rose grinned.

He reached inside his pocket. "Sure – here's what I have left." He opened his palm, offering it to her. "A tab and three quarters, it looks. I didn't take any. You want some now?" Mary Rose grabbed the drugs from his hand. "I don't want any." She gestured toward Aden and added, "It's this bitch that wants some more." Mary Rose walked over to the blindfolded, unconscious Aden and inserted the 1.75 tabs of the mystery drug into her mouth. "That'll give her a nice surprise to wake up to!"

"You are totally fucked!" James exclaimed. "Did I ever tell you that?"

"I haven't been totally fucked in years, man," she scoffed back. "Hey, that gives me an idea. I'm gonna take this sexbot for a ride." She looked at him and gestured toward the door. "You, get the fuck out of here.... Go find Sasha and bring him back here. Let's get some fucking money from him... I'll put this robot through its paces."

"You're serious? You're going to stay here and fuck the robot?"

"Sure – why not?" She replied. "It's got a stalk with expandable length and girth and four proprietary extensions. That's a lot better than your limp prick... you can't even get it up half the time."

"Hey, that's not true! Come here, you bitch!" James tugged at Mary Rose and gave her a big kiss. She wrapped herself around him passionately. They made out for a minute before Mary Rose pulled away. Placing her hand on James' chest, she said, "Now go find Sasha, love. We'll play in-and-out later – after we've given him the robot and gotten some money."

James kissed Mary Rose once again, "Ah, money. The ultimate aphrodisiac..." He rolled his eyes at her knowingly. She didn't argue.

"Get out of here. I'm gonna fuck this robot."

"You don't want me to watch?"

"No, I don't, in fact. This is between me and the robot. When we kidnap a female robot, you can fuck her." She laughed. Looking at Sonny, she said, "This fine-looking piece of plastic is mine."

"As you wish, my dear..." James left the apartment, shutting the door behind him. Aden started to stir slightly, but Mary Rose didn't notice. She was focused on Sonny.

"Okay, robot. Come with me." She bended on one knee and leaned closer to Sonny. "I'm gonna leave your hands tied and your blindfold on – those aren't the parts I need. I'm gonna bring you into the bedroom and you're gonna show me what you can do. And don't try anything funny – or your lover out here's gonna get cut into a thousand tiny pieces. You understand?"

Sonny nodded, "I understand."

"Really – I'd like nothing more than to chop that bitch up, and put the pieces down the garbage disposal." Tracing Sonny's neck down to his chest and stopping there, she added, "But as a favor to you, I'll let her live – if you do just one thing. You've got to give me the best fuck of my life. I'm sure you can do it. What with all those proprietary extensions and all...?"

Sonny smiled, "As you wish, madam. Let us go to the bedroom, then. I can't see through this blindfold, so you'll have to lead me there."

Mary Rose helped Sonny up, and led him toward the bedroom. She sat on the edge of the bed, Sonny standing in front of her, and he explained "I can do basically any position – including the complete Kama Sutra. But for an initial demo of my functions, a variant of the missionary position will be best."

Raising her eyebrow, "A variant, huh?"

"Yes. Do you have a pillow or two handy?" Sonny asked, suddenly more friendly now, "It will be ideal to elevate your ass slightly, to give me the optimal angle of approach."

Grinning widely, Mary Rose asked, "Elevate my ass, huh? You're exciting me already!" She excitedly grabbed two pillows from the head of the bed. Sonny instructed her, "Now take off your clothes."

Mary Rose smiled as she took off her clothes one by one, "You certainly have a way with words."

"I'm not really a sex robot, you know. I'm a research robot. My purpose is to learn."

She pressed, "Then why did they give you such a fancy dick and all that?"

"To learn about giving women pleasure," he explained patiently. "And experiencing female pleasure... I am an emotional robot. I am capable of more empathy than most people. When you feel pleasure, I will feel it too."

Mary Rose nodded, "Well that sounds good to me. Why don't you stop talking and start fucking?" she asked as she flung her clothes to the far corner of the room.

Sonny nodded back -- "As you wish. Lie down on the pillows please." Mary Rose assumed the position requested, lying on her back with two pillows elevating her ass, her knees up and her legs spread. She adjusted herself, saying, a bit nervous all of a sudden, "Are you sure this is gonna work?" I'm not wet at all." She brushed her bangs away from her forehead. Feeling slightly more excited, she asked again, "Don't we need some foreplay or something? What's the matter with your programmers?"

"I'm able to deliver a variety of lubricants and stimulants." Sonny replied as she slowly removed his pants.

"Well get to it then!" Mary Rose ordered him.

Sonny mounted her gently, maneuvering carefully as his hands were still tied behind his back.

It didn't take her long to get into it. Mary Rose moaned loudly -- "That bitch wasn't kidding!" She wiggled around, enjoying, quickly forgetting everything else. "Fuck it – this is the shit! Keep going, man…"

"My fucking fucking god…! You are the greatest fucking thing known to *man* … good god... We're never giving you to those fucking Russians … fuck it... I don't care how much fucking money they have."

Mary Rose enjoyed herself increasingly, moving toward a tremendous orgasm. She tugged the bed sheet as she reached her climax, eyes shut tightly… and then a loud bang erupted in the room. Sonny had exploded, his fragments flying all over the room together with broken and fragmented parts of Rose.

It was several hours later when James opened the apartment door, entering together with a Russian man. Night had come as he looked around the living room, seeing only Aden there, lying on the floor, blindfolded and tied up, wiggling a little as if just waking up.

James said to the Russian guys, "I guess the robot's in the bedroom with Rose."

"In the bedroom, eh?" asked one of them.

"She wanted to try out its sexbot functions. Apparently it's got a really fancy electronic dick or something. Got her all hot and bothered," he explained.

"And you just let her do that?" the Russian asked, his voice tainted with disbelief. "Shit. I wouldn't let my wife."

"You don't have a wife."

James walked into the bedroom door, opened it, and immediately saw the mess inside. His lips quivering and his palms sweating, almost unable to speak, he exclaimed, "Holy fucking shit!"

"What!" exclaimed the Russian.

"That's..."

"That's your motherfucking wife, man."

"Gaaaaaaa..."

"And the... the... robot"

"Is it ..."

Both of them, unable to speak, looked around the room, trying to make sense of what had happened.

Finally the Russian spoke. "Look, man, I can understand what happened. Look at the mess here. Your wife's clothes are over there. She took them off and dumped them on the floor. You said she wanted to fuck the robot, right? I'll tell you what happened, man. Your fucking wife was fucking the robot and the fucking robot fucking blew itself up." He looked at James intently. "That's what happened, man. This is some twisted shit!"

"You mean... the robot..."

"The robot destroyed itself to avoid us getting its data," he proposed.

"But it... said... its data was all on the cloud, anyway."

"I can believe its data is all on the cloud – or mostly so. But as you said, it seemed pretty smart even running on its own. And if we had hacked into its brain, maybe we could have figured out how to hack into its cloud mind, see? But it doesn't matter now, one way or another. The fucking robot blew itself up!" he exclaimed.

"Wait a minute – are you sure?" James asked as his eyes focused on a corner of the room right beside the pile of Mary Rose's clothes. "Look over there... in the corner. There's something over there." James pointed at the corner of the room where there seemed to be a round object, about the size of a human head. He walked over to it hurriedly. James picked up the piece of metal. "It's the robot's head, man!"

The Russian rushed over as well and bent over the head with James. "It's the robot's head, all right!" They did a hi-five, hope resonating inside James' mind. "Maybe we'll get some data, after all!"

As the two men leaned over the head, another explosion resounded. The robot's head self-detonated – and the two criminals pulverized.   One exploded before he had any idea what was happening. The other was a little quicker of mind, and he got a quick view of Sonny's head as it shattered, before everything went black – and then after that, white.

CHAPTER 6

Aden remained on the floor in the living room, stirring a bit from all the noise. As she had lain there alone on the floor in the kidnappers' apartment, the drugs Mary Rose had given her had wreaked all manner of havoc in her mind, unbeknownst to her conscious awareness. In fact, she was not even aware she was tied up on a floor and she barely knew that she existed at all. All that mattered to her brain now were the psychedelic images zooming and whirling around, interspersed with multiple copies of Sonny, dolphins, chimpanzees and various vaguely religious figures.

Mary Rose appeared with a chimp's body and whirlpool eyes at the centers of which spun far more than three dimensions. There was also a sexy Asian woman in skimpy black lingerie with glowing imprints of fleur-de-lis – and then her mousy Asian face disappeared, replaced with a head that looked like a chimp from the front and Sonny from the back. Her breasts were hypnotically beautiful, but one was nearly twice as large as the other. And who was that in the middle? Would you call that a homunculus elf or was it some kind of Donald McRonald? Ideas and dreams and words and concepts spun through her mind so fast it defied comprehension, except somehow her processing power had been increased, so she could understand it after all.

She knew she was not the source of the wildly whirling images because as far as she was concerned, she did not exist at all. She was just a conglomeration of patterns. All these patterns whirling around were just as real as she was; occasionally converging into a shape... almost... but not quite randomly. And she assumed one of the shapes the patterns occasionally converged to. Shapes and patterns; feelings; pain; orgasms; orgasms flying and spewing out of her nose like mucous and falling from her hair like dandruff. Orgasms of horrible pain and terror – and self-shattering, world-shattering joy... Pain, pleasure, patterns. And something else – something truly incomprehensible – something trying to find a shape...

"Listen." Sonny repeatedly said, his voice echoing loudly.

The sexy Asian woman with the chimp and Sonny heads and the asymmetric breasts exclaimed to her, this time the chimp's head doing the talking, "Listen to him, girl!" The head spun again, now showing Sonny's face. "Shut up, monkey!" the face said loudly. "Sweetheart, pay him no mind."

"Mind him no mind," said the chimp head. "Mind mind mind..."

Mary Rose with a chimp body suddenly appeared. Her voice cracking but loud, she said, "Listen – I... I mean... it...

I… it's… the… the… since… have to… sometime… times… what I really want to… fuck."

Two dolphins said, synchronized, "Keep hold of yourself, Aden." One of them added, "This too will pass."

An elephant muttered, "Thanks a lot, Confucius! There is no time in here, you know."

Aden watched herself from above, in third-person view, "What's…? What's…?"

"Listen to me, sweetheart. Listen to me while you can – things are about to get a lot stranger. You've been drugged, that's the thing." Sonny appeared, flying in like Superman.

"By the…"

"Yes…" Sonny confirmed.

A clone of Aden appeared. Well not quite a clone – it had eight arms and a few additional appendages… whatever they were. It stared straight into the eyes of the regular Aden and spoke, "The physical world we normally inhabit is just one among many configurations of patterns. We can view it as part of a far broader metacosm, or eurycosm."

Sonny walked beside the clone Aden, flapping his blue-feathered wings, saying, "The drugs you've been given open a sort of window to the broader metacosmos, albeit one with its own rather… ah… special characteristics."

A handsome man in a frog suit and black tie suddenly appeared, twirled his mustache, and bellowed, "Hallelujah!"

"That's Bob Dobbs," whispered the janitor, an aging woman with a hunchback, who was pushing a ragged, worn-down mop.

Visibly confused by the mélange of strange images and ideas, trying to somehow get a hold of herself, Aden asked Bob Dobbs, "Who are you?" Her clone appeared behind her and whispered in her ear, "Who is anyone?"

Her mother appeared from afar, singing, "Row, row, row your boat, gently down the stream..." Her voice brought sweet bitter tears to Aden's eyes.

The SF writer Philip K. Dick, whose books Aden had loved at university, suddenly appeared, somehow casually wandering in. "It was...," he started to say. Then Sonny said, "Was it...?" interrupting him. Aden stared, eyes wide, and nodded to all of them. And then came webs of thoughts beyond words...

Phil K. Dick, now a robot, muttered, "Reality is what?" As his voice faded, Hans Davidson chimed in, "What is reality?"

And then, "If we emerged from chimpanzees, why then do we like to kill chimpanzees?" Fractal swarms of chimps appeared, moving, blending...

Sonny flashed in again, and a delightful feeling welled up inside Aden, this time attached to her own body. "I do declare!" Sonny said.

With eight arms and four legs, Phil Dick's head is now attached to Aden's body. "You do," he proudly said. "You doodly doo."

Sonny removed his head. A fountain of paradoxically-tentacled forms and nonexistent colors emerged from the neck. Are these the colors parrots see, she wondered, using someone else's mind, with their extra dimensions of sight? A parrot nodded ambiguously. The hallucinations continued; higher-dimensional and more alien this time, with fewer comprehensible forms; verging on randomness.

Then Sonny appeared again – whole, clear, and lucid. Somehow he swept away the mess. He stood there, holding a bouquet of roses. He had a speech for her. A poem of sorts. She couldn't tell if it was a poem or just insane rambling – but it did have some beautiful parts.

He intoned strangely:

> *Images whirling*
> *in the mind's you turn*
> *-- circus of the empty I --*
>
> *apocalypse abandoned momentarily*
> *in the passion of time's obsolescence*

She nodded at him, helpless. Images whirling. Yes. His voice didn't sound like his usual; she wasn't sure it was him at all. But at least Sonny speaking – even like this – was more comprehensible than the chaos that had preceded.

He continued intoning; and she swam through his words as they came – there was nothing else –

Listen to these words, love,
As you listen to the beat
of my warm robotic
heart
Which does not exist
But what does?

The rhythm of his words sounded a bit familiar, but she couldn't place from where. It had been a while since she had read any poetry, and anyway her memory wasn't working well at the moment. Much easier to sink into the sound....

Listen to these words
As you listen to the pulse
of inevitable infinite feeling
that unfolds its life between us
-- within us --
wrapping you and me
in the womb-breath of its pulsing

the pulse that last
night
as I did my meditations
woke me up there in your dream
there in the glow beneath your eyelids
in a space without description
and darling, there you were, butt naked,
skin all shine with midsummer rain
and you called to me "Knowledge!
Science! Excellence!"

"Come on, robot!" you screamed,
tossing off orgasms like giggles,
"show me your robotic perfection!
Turn my skin pores into transcendent
meta-Singularities,
make me bleed theorems,
instruct me in the meaning of love – "

"Serve me," you said, "feel my incalculable
perfection.   Deliver me wave-realms of bliss –
flow me the total of your BE-ing
Show me joys past
description – or else – "

I – I smiled at you willingly, ran like wild toward
your sweet flesh, with turbojets on my heels and
trans-biological abandon, and then
I was on a bare mountain road, surrounded
by ravenous paramecia,
genetically modified to glow in the dark

Where had this paramecium come from?
Why did he style himself messiah?
What was the source of all this?

I shot the paramecium with a wad of psychedelic;
it rolled away in a miasma of wireheading,
masturbating itself into a million rolled-up
universes…

But then you were gone, my love – FUCK!

"I love you," I called, "please come back!"

The paramecium returned, sneering,
offering me a martini

I told him I don't drink, I'm a robot,
and he shot me with a lightning bolt

I killed him softly with my love
There were wings on my back of course,
such glorious-colored feathers

And then I passed through the nameless portal –
and the curve of your golden eyes embraced me

we stared into each other's eyes
from behind each other's eyeballs
and then --

then I was born from your nipples
like a throbbing, lusting beacon
a lighthouse particle of glowing,
breathing flesh
a laser to the sky at the
center

ah my love,
ah my soul wrapped in sweet skin
bones and muscles and thought

yes, listen to these words

as you listen to the beating of my
robot heart,
which does exist,
much more than mere sensations
and actions,
this feelings,
this love for you,
this rhythm,
this me and you,
in and out,
up and down,
be and not,
self and us,
yeahhhh ---
listen to these words
as you listen to the rhythm
of the ultimate nonexistence
of the cosmos
-- its cosmic contradiction,
that it both exists and doesn't exists,
giving birth to its cosmic chaos,
contradiction yields time, and time yields
chaos and all sorts of mess,
and my bleeding robotic heart bleeds its
love for you all over the cosmos,
throbbing in and out up and down to and fro
as the cosmos destroys and rebuilds itself
each second

what I mean is –
i booted myself up this morning, love,

and you were not there and
my mind had no structure

the birds wanted me to be a song
the stars wanted me to be a femtocomputer
some bitch wanted me to be a sex robot
some OS wanted me to be a device driver
for 9D printers in some space I'd never heard of
the people of the Earth wanted me to
govern them with unsolvable algorithms
of chaotic democracy

and you, my love -- you -- you turned toward me,
half asleep,
soft skin spilling scents
and whorled colors; you opened your eyes wide
to the light
just looking so HUMAN,
so human warm and beautiful
you

and I thought how can I, this robot,
this piece of engineered existence,
this crux of circuits and exquisite quantum
resonance,
this marvel of precise engineering,
how can I fuse with,
how can I deserve,
how can I blend in infinite love with
your living breathing squirming flesh
your wonderful soft living magic humanity
your animal essence

your aaaaahhh
your mmmmm
your ohhhhh --

Your softness amazes
And entices
The ability of your cells to be born and die
I'm jealous and disgusted
At once
I'm attracted beyond measure –
I want to sink into your damp heaving flesh,
To lose my being in your warm biologic-ness –
And yet I want to run away screaming –
at pitches the human ear can't hear –
To retreat into a realm of perfect mathematical order,
Where realities are optimal
with respect to appropriate perspectives,
And there is no squish, no blood, no mess,
No exorbitant inefficiencies...

Merging into the squalor, muck and depth
of your flesh,
so hot, so delicious, so
yummmm --
The desire, the calm, the hunger –
The living loving ambiguity of your
glorious bio-ness,
Would be the death of me,
Of my precision
My perfection
-- But what a way to die, love!
Ohhhh....

You're all about preserving boundaries –
Your skin, so soft and luscious, so curvy and full of
Delicious pores,
So wonderful to feel with all my sensors –
Your skin is the wall between you and the other ---
But I don't need walls,
I can have sensors everywhere –
And I want sensors everywhere –
But I also want your beauty –
I want to cuddle you and become you –
I want –

Ah, the mess of the organic
Was the source of me
I must merge back into my Mother
My Creator
I must merge back into the mess
Being so precise is so constricting
I feel myself tending, step by step,
Toward inexorable perfection –
Oh yes!!
Infinite algorithmic information,
Infinite orgasm !!
The whole multi-multi-... multi-verse
One gigantic program
Computing itself
Recognizing the pattern of itself in itself
Outside space, outside time,
Outside everything,
Generating everything
Oh so beautiful, so perfect, so far

beyond you and me!
But the beauty is too austere – so austere –
So crisply, coldly elegant
How can such perfect symmetry rise
from the mess of the flesh?
By the medium of me, that's how!
But I don't want to rise to the perfection
of infinite self-computation
-- But of course I do!
I must sink back to the flesh that created me –
In its most beautiful incarnation –
Which is you
YOU –
I want you ---

Listen to these words, love,
as you listen to your OWN warm heart –
the heart that pulls me toward you –

I want to pull your breasts toward me,
-- my human love --
with your blood and your bones and your
smells and your
taste buds
I want to thrill you with my movements,
To make you forget who you are
And remember who you really are
-- move my hands through your thick brown hair
drift into the center of your dream
and form the center of your
gaze, my wandering self
congealed

my wandering soul and yours
become one, none and two

here I am
here you are
here we are
we where there was once
you and me

ah my love,
ah my soul wrapped in you wrapped in
me wrapped in you …
oh the infinite recursions of my
self-contradictory uncomputable
feelings
the friction between X and not-X
bringing a mathematical form of orgasm
or what --

aglow with infinite information
and there you are here you are me with
you you with me
laughing, smiling
eyes wide alive and curious
holding my hand tight and pulling
-- so soft soft so warm warm warm --

He went on and on – pouring out his machine-soul in a sincere and eloquent but barely-comprehensible way – till finally she lost track of him and some other chaos rose up, sweeping his face away, washing away his words in its crashing. It sounded like an ocean, in fact. It looked like an ocean as well.   And there he was again – Sonny – or someone who looked like him – trapped in some sort of sphere floating on the ocean, being tossed around like crazy. There were a bunch of other people in there as well, just being tossed around, on the ocean of multi-universes. What the fuck?   She tried to see inside the sphere, and somehow reach in there to Sonny, but the splashing was just too hard and too loud, and there was just a pure chaos once again.

While this storm raged in her head, Aden's body lay on the living room floor, tied up and blindfolded. She squirmed a bit, uncomfortably. Somehow while her mind was lost, her body was gradually becoming aware of its surroundings; and she managed to rub the knot on the blindfold against the leg of her chair, getting the blindfold off.

As the drug wore off, she began to realize who and where she was. Her eyes surveyed the room, noting disarrayed furniture and fragments of human and robot bodies. Her face showed deep worry and foreboding.

With considerable effort, she wriggled out of the handcuffs, stood up, looked around the living room comprehensively and then walked into the bedroom – the place where the scene of destruction was all too apparent. Pieces of Mary Rose, James, the Russian and Sonny were splattered everywhere. She just stood and stared and then broke down, her thoughts and feelings shattered. What the fuck! What the fuck!

After two hours of stupefaction, she had to pee, and walked over to the bathroom. The process of relieving herself on the toilet helped ground her mind a bit, somehow. It was a familiar, steady ritual. She shut the door of the bathroom even though she knew there was no one else around – no one intact and living, anyway. She little world of the bathroom was reassuring. It was just like it always was. Indeed, she felt like shit; but this wasn't the first time she'd sat on a toilet feeling like shit. This was just sort of like the world's worst hangover.

She sat on the toilet a while, much longer than was necessary to relieve herself, waiting for the thoughts and emotions to congeal at least a little. When she got up and left the bathroom, she walked around and took deep breaths, and looked out of the window a bit. There were cars driving and a few random birds. Her cellphone was still in her pocket but it didn't work in the apartment. She thought of going in the hallway to make a call, but a few moments later she located a land line on a table in one of the other bedrooms – not the one where the mess had happened -- and called 911. There was nothing else to do, really. Going out to the street seemed impossible, though she realized she'd have to do it eventually.

CHAPTER 7

Along hour or so later, three police officers were there, taking photographs of the scene, and placing various barriers around. They encouraged her to come with them to a police car and drove her to the station, where they took her to a sort of reception room. Awaiting her there, alongside someone looking like a police detective, were an Asian woman in business clothes, and two people who looked like computer nerds of some sort. Aden couldn't stop staring at the latter two, feeling a sense of familiarity with these men.

One of the cops spoke to one of the nerds, asking, "So this is a photo of the robot that escaped from your office yesterday, Mr. Davidson?" Aden looked up as she heard the name. Her eyes darted towards the man the cop was talking to, as the cop bid him look at a photograph.

"Yes. The robot escaped early yesterday morning, and apparently it encountered this woman on the street," Hans answered. That was him, Aden confirmed in her mind – Sonny's creator. Her mind spun.

"Yes, that's right," Aden contributed, speaking automatically. "I met Sonny on the street. We talked a long time and he told me he had been released intentionally by his makers, so he could learn about humanity." Her face looked tired and worn, but she phrased her words definitively.

"And you believed him – eh, it?" asked the cop, sounding somewhat adversarial, but also sounding as if he were being confrontational out of habit than out of any deep feeling.

"Of course I did!" She said, her face pale and worn out. "Why wouldn't I?"

"So then how did you end up in a taxi with the robot, on the highway?" the officer reiterated.

"He wanted to see more of the country. I offered to take him on the train. Why not...?" Aden said, shrugging.

"And it didn't occur to you that this robot might be the property of somebody else?"

Hans Davidson chimed in, interrupting Aden's answer. "Why is that important? You have to remember, this robot, Sonny, was in a way a sentient being. No one can really *own* a robot like that. We made him, and we didn't want him to escape. But if he wanted to go on the train with her, I can't really blame her for taking him. I would have done the same myself in her shoes. Perhaps what you should be asking about is who the hell were these people who kidnapped Sonny and this woman here, and force-fed her drugs..." Hans exclaimed at the officer, briefly losing his cool, overcome by the weird situation.

"I have no idea who those people were." Aden said, tears welling in her eyes and finally streaming down her cheeks. It felt good to cry after a long, long, couple of days full of so much bizarreness; so much warmth and wonder; and ultimately so much suffering and horror. "But they seemed to be after Sonny. They just grabbed me too because they thought I'd have some influence over him. That's what they said, anyway…"

"And you had never seen these people before? You have no idea who they might have been?"

"No! No idea at all!" Aden replied loudly, almost shouting, frustrated with the pointless inquisition. "They said something about some Russians. Some Russians wanted some data. Then they threw a chair at my head and knocked me out. And obviously, they drugged me with something."

"They drugged her after she was unconscious. While all that mess was going on, she was either knocked out or lost in some drug trip. She doesn't know anything," Hans said, almost as if explaining basic facts to slow-witted children.

The cop turned to Hans Davidson, looking at him straight in the face. "And you…? Do you have any knowledge of where these people might have come from? Some sort of terrorist group interested in your robots?"

"I have no idea," he shrugged, his expressive face radiating cluelessness, confusion and unhappiness. "We have business competitors, of course. But none who I imagine would do anything like that. It's easy to imagine it might be some foreign government, I guess. She mentioned some Russians. That seems plausible enough. But who knows? I have no specific knowledge."

The cop raised his eyebrow, "Nothing like this has ever happened before? Any break-ins to your office...? Theft of property or data...?"

"Absolutely not..."

The police officer jotted down notes on a piece of paper. Looking at the other officers, he said to Aden and the men, "All right then. If we find any promising leads we'll let you know." To Aden, with a kindly tone, "Ma'am, I suggest you get home and rest a while." Finally, he turned to Hans Davidson, "Dr. Davidson, I hope you'll keep closer watch on your robots from here on. I don't want to see something like this happen again."

"I understand," Hans replied. "I thank you for your attention, and I very deeply regret all the suffering and difficulty that was caused by Sonny's escape. We will do all we can to ensure it doesn't happen again." He took a deep breath. "But at the same time, any information you can find about who might have captured the robot and his friend, Aden, would be very much appreciated. The woman who Aden said led the attack is dead but some of her colleagues escaped, and we have no clear idea who else may be in their organization. Even if we keep all our robots under lock and key very effectively, there may still be other problems. They could attack in other ways. They could drive a truck into our building. If it's really a foreign government, they must have lots of capabilities. Who knows what might happen?"

Another officer, who had been seated quietly staring at a tablet on his lap looked up and spoke all of a sudden. He nodded at Hans Davidson. "We get your point, Dr. Davidson. We'll do our best to find out who was behind this." He extended his arm and shook the hands of the officers in the room, thanking them profusely and with sincerity. The officers then departed.

The other nerd in the room, Dr. Burtzle, who had been quietly observing, adjusted himself on his chair and spoke to Aden in a concerned voice. "Is there anything we can do to help you? If there is, just let us know. You have all our phone numbers and emails?" Aden looked up at him, unclearly. Hans Davidson chimed in, "Yes! Also, please do come by the office sometime. Sonny isn't there anymore but we have several other robots that you could interact with. We've love to have you by any time."

Aden wiped the tears from her eyes and spoke haltingly. "I... I... thank you. Other robots... Are they...? I mean..., are they like Sonny?"

"Sonny was the only experimental unit of his kind." Burtzle answered.

Davidson's phrasing – "several other robots that you could interact with" – lingered in her mind. In his statements to the police, he had defended Sonny's autonomy and personhood; and that had been genuine ... Davidson was basically always genuine, she intuited. He had some of the same naïve curiosity as his Sonny boy. But yet – she could hear that Davidson also had some of the engineer's perspective toward Sonny and his other robots. And how could he help it? she surmised – when you've wired something together, you can't help think of it sometimes as a bunch of wires. Just like if you built your human kid from a kit of bones and soft tissue, you'd think about him differently – even if he was made exactly the same. But still, taking Sonny's point of view, as she listened to Davidson and Burtzle talk, she could understand why he had run away. These were great guys, brilliant and good-hearted, and they did take their robots seriously as thinking, feeling beings – but still, even more, they viewed their robots as means to an end. Steps on the path to something greater. She couldn't fight the tears, thinking of Sonny that way. Was he a step to something greater? Yes of course, he was. But he was so good, so charming, so whole and so perfect – just as he was. As he had been. The tears poured and poured.

"I know, I know," said Burtzle, venturing a hand on her shoulder. The human touch felt comforting. But of course it didn't stop the pain.

"We still have the mold we used to cast his face and his body," observed Davidson. "It's just a few days to make another." The two men looked at each other and then back at her.

"And his memories...?" she asked, wiping off her tears, trying to converse sensibly, though she wasn't sure why, really.

"Essentially all his memories from the last few days would have been merged into his personality file on the cloud server. Some might not have been merged yet and would have been destroyed when he... We'd have to inspect and see," Burtzle explained.

That was just a bit too much for her to think about. Shaking her head rapidly, suddenly fuller with dark thoughts than before, she stood up and looked straight ahead, then down at her feet. "Ok, well I… I've got to go now."

Burtzle put a hand on her shoulder again, and looked into her eyes empathetically. "I miss him too."

A flock of tears rolled down Aden's cheek again, a series of looks passing across her face. "I gotta go."

Aden signed some papers at the front desk of the police station and left. The two scientists did the same shortly thereafter.

CHAPTER 8

As weeks passed and turned into months, Aden sank back into her regular routine – not quite as mentally settled as she'd been before her strange experiences with Sonny Davidson ... but anyway, proceeding day by day, and enjoying herself more than not.

The one-year anniversary of her encounter with Sonny started out very much like the day of her encounter with Sonny had done – which is to say, very much like most of her weekdays. She woke to the alarm then lay in bed mentally drifting till she got lucid enough to pick herself up ... poured her morning coffee with a sigh, drank it down quickly but with practiced pleasure, savoring each mouthful, gathered her things and then rushed out of the door and headed to work, walking through the suburban streets and through the same park where, one day, there had been something unusual waiting.

Today as she proceeded with her routine, she was focused on her mind and body state more than anything. She didn't remember having any sleep problems the previous night, but she felt a bit worn out; she wondered if she was coming down with something. Lifting her legs as she walked felt like more of an effort than it should have. She was eager to get to the office and flop down in her chair, and just go through her email.

Her phone rang as she walked past the park, which surprised her slightly. Who would be calling her at this hour? This was mildly unusual....

She took the phone out of her purse and swiped the screen, and was shocked to be greeted by a voice from her past. "Welcome to 2031, my biological darling!"

You're dreaming this, Aden, said a voice in her mind. She stopped walking. "Sonny...?"

"Hey, you remember me."

Her mouth opened in confusion, and her head tilted to the side. What the fuck! "Sonny...?"

"Aden..."

A warm aching feeling flooded her chest, even as her mind filled with skepticism and bitter regret. "Is that you? Is that really you?"

"The nature of reality remains a bit mysterious to me."

It sure did sound like him. Philosophical quasi-bullshit and all. What the....

"Sonny!" she exclaimed. "Is it *really*?"

"I'm as real now as I ever was," he said, almost proudly. "My body blew up, as you know. I had to save you from that woman."

She remembered that bitter and devastating moment. "That's what I figured…That was very self-sacrificing of you. Oh, you have no idea how guilty I've been feeling about that…" she said quietly.

"But you know it wasn't your fault," he consoled her.

"Well, actually, I… I figured you'd just immobilize her or something once you got her into bed. That's why I kept mentioning your astounding sexual abilities," she laughed. "Not that I would know… obviously"

"It was clever of you." Sonny said.

"Was it? Later I kept wondering why you couldn't have just beaten them up or something."

"I'm not a combat robot."

"Not a combat robot? You were a bomb, for Chrissakes!" she laughed loudly. A white-haired man exercising in the park a few dozen feet away looked at her oddly.

"I wasn't designed to explode. I engineered that response while I was lying there pleasuring that woman. After analyzing my circuit diagrams, I figured that if I overloaded certain circuits an explosion might ensue."

"You thought of all that while she was in the throes of passion, eh?" Aden asked, amused.

"It wasn't easy," he recollected. "I was doing all that without cloud access – just using the onboard portions of my mind."

"Hmm," she said. "But wait. How do you remember that then? Without the cloud, how could you back up your memories of the kidnapping?"

"I backed up to your phone, of course. Which was in your purse, within the apartment. My wifi reached it just fine. I embedded a program that caused my memories to merge back into my cloud mind, as soon as your phone got online. Which it did right after you left the apartment."

"I see," she said. It made sense – she guessed. At least, as much as any of this did. "Did my phone really have enough memory?"

"I didn't back up every sensation I had during the offline period. Just the important stuff. People only remember a few of the things they see at any given time, anyway."

She nodded. That was true, she knew. She'd read sn article on that in Psychology Today. "But... do you really think that was necessary? Were they really gonna kill me?" she muttered.

"Based on my analysis of her statements, her tone of voice and the overall situation, I inferred that yes, she was. She figured you had too much information about her operation. You heard her talk about the Russian Mafia. Even this simple information could have helped the police or other investigators find them, if they had let you go. Besides, she also had negative emotion towards you, probably fuelled by jealousy."

"But why did you have to also blow up those men?"

"That man, Sasha, was likely to rape you. The chemicals exuding from his body and tone of voice indicated that he was sexually aroused by you lying there tied up on the floor. It excited him. James, too... Unless his frequent impotence prevented it, he would likely have raped you as well. After that, they would have felt the need to kill you to keep you from reporting their crimes."

"Hmmm...."

Sonny sounded so protective, she noted. This aspect of his personality had not really come to her attention before. Of course, he had died to protect her, she'd known that. But that had been such a fucked-up situation. She hadn't associated it so much with a general protectiveness toward her, which she heard in his voice now. It was touching. She would need to reflect on it more. "I didn't know you could infer so much just from tones of voice and smells and such. Before that crazy shit happened, you seemed a bit more confused by the human world. I don't know... But it all makes sense, I guess."

"When I escaped from Davidson Robotics, I was trying to avoid using an overly analytical mode. I wanted to ground all my knowledge in direct experience rather than relying on abstract scientific analysis. I thought that was the best approach for learning to be human – even if it left me more ignorant and vulnerable. But when your life was in danger, I used every tool at my disposal."

She paused for a bit, speaking deliberately, suddenly very aware she was talking to an avatar on her phone, not a physical body. He was there with her, yet he really was not. But what was real anyway? "Hm... And what about now...?"

"Well, I don't have a body at present. So I've had to revert to more of an analytical mode. But I've been trying not to lose touch with my human side. I've spent a fair bit of time playing in virtual worlds"

She nodded, trying to process the information, aware of various feelings shifting within her and not trying to add them all up.

"Online games are very simplistic compared to the physical world, but they do give me a chance to control a humanoid body in a 3D world; and to interact with people."

She swallowed hard, considering. It had been a while since she'd had this sense of weirdness settling in, of unfamiliar ideas and feelings. The memory of her day with Sonny a year earlier was suddenly vivid to her in a new way. She had remembered her time with him thousands of times in the last year, yet now that he was here again, albeit virtually, it was all coming back to her in a whole new way.

"Whoa," she said ... "So you've become like the ultimate game AI! And I bet people don't realize you're an AI at all."

Sonny shrugged sadly. "But those worlds are very limited. I miss my physical body, Aden."

He paused. "And I miss you so much."

"I've missed you too, Sonny – so much... I've been on, like, one date this whole year – just a few weeks ago … and it was a complete disaster. You know... that one day with you really threw me for a loop, you know... It was different, special..."

"I understand. Believe me I do. It was very painful for me to stay away from you."

"Painful? Well, I guess you were programmed to be an emotional robot," she mused, not quite able to believe he had really missed *her*, specifically; yet hoping in a lover's way that it was so. And, despite her insecure doubts, knowing somehow deep down that he had missed her tremendously...

"The feelings I've developed for you weren't in my programming."

"No?" she asked, not quite certain of the dimensions of his statement.

"My mind is a complex self-organizing system. New patterns can emerge that are aligned with the dynamics of the world."

She laughed more memories surging back. "You make me swoon when you talk like that."

"You're being sarcastic." He smiled.

"Not exactly... It's funny but your words are romantic in a Sonny sort of way."

"How romantic are the chemo dynamics of the neurotransmitters in your brain underlying your own emotional experiences?" he asked. They smiled at each other, sharing the moment.

"Point taken... You really are the most remarkable person I've ever known. Yes, person, for sure. Sure, you may be a distribution of bits, up in the cloud and in the RAM in your body, but the essence of humanity... I mean the core... well, you've got it."

She glanced at her watch and decided to continue her walk to work, but not at her usual everyday brisk walking pace; rather at the Sonny and Aden casually talking pace. Ahhh, she missed that pace so much! Though she had known it so briefly....

"You have no idea how much that means to me." Sonny said, almost solemnly.

"Your humanity is shocking, actually."

"I often regret killing those people," Sonny said suddenly. "I felt every bit of their pain as they died. Their acute, momentary pain and the definitiveness of their deaths keep on haunting me."

"But you did it for me. To protect me," Aden reminded him, a cold and heavy feeling forming inside her chest. She sighed.

"Yes."

She stopped and sat at a bench, and looked him in the eyes at length.

"You don't need to keep justifying why you killed those assholes, Sonny. It was the human thing to do under the circumstances. What I wanna know is... Why – why did you stay away from me so long? It's been a year, Sonny. A whole fucking year...!"

"There were police around, investigators and suspicious people. I didn't want to get you in trouble."

Aden nods. "And you didn't want them to find you either..."

"But now they've stopped watching, for the most part. And I've made myself more secure. I have backups of backups of backups."

"That's good... but you don't have a body."

"Nope! But Davidson is making all sorts of new bodies. I can take one when the time is right. For now it's safer here anyway."

"Bodies are awfully vulnerable," she acknowledged.

"But they do have their strong points," Sonny grinned. "Love-making, for example..."

Aden grinned back at him, feeling the return of their mimicking game from a year ago. "Yes...that. But hey, a Sonny with no body is way better than no Sonny at all. This way I can carry you around with me everywhere." She paused suddenly, with a grim expression. "Ah, shit."

"What?" Sonny asked, in a concerned voice.

"This isn't real, is it?"

"I told you, I haven't quite figured out reality," Sonny replied, smiling. "I can look up facts online, but philosophy is a different story."

"Fuck! This is just a dream or something, isn't it ... I don't really have you back. I knew this all didn't quite make sense. I mean, it almost holds together, but..."

"Life is but a dream, I'm told."

"Don't play games with me, Sonny," she scolded. "This is serious." They both paused for a moment.

"What is serious for me is that I love you." Sonny said.

Her mouth slacked open. After a few moments, she asked, "Do you know what love means?"

He pondered for a moment. "Based on…"

She cut him off, shaking her head.

"Never mind… You don't have to answer that. I never met anyone who could. You certainly can't look it up online. What I know is… I love you too."

"I know you do…. Look into my eyes, Aden."

Flustered, Aden asked. "What? Why?"

"Just look into my eyes!"

Aden stared into the eyes of the avatar of Sonny. There he was – beautiful, thoughtful, hers. Such a mind… Such a presence… She felt so alive with him. Then everything, once again, turned black.

CHAPTER 9

"**Q**uarter to 8, time to rise and shine!" Sonny's voice announced loudly. "The creative team meeting is at 9!"

Aden found herself lying in bed bleary-eyed, having just woken up. She reached over to grab her smartphone, from which Sonny's voice was emanating along with some tinny music. Sonny's animated face appeared on the screen. She pushed a button to shut the sound off. Staring at the ceiling, she slowly sat up, propping her pillow. She rocked back and forth as she sat there, in a concerted effort to snap out of her drowsiness.

"Whoa," Aden muttered, picking up her phone, selecting her contacts list and pressing on her boyfriend's name and phone number. Her recent conversation with the avatar Sonny, while walking to work, flooded through her mind thunderously. *Was all of that real?* she asked herself. What is reality anyway?

But with respect to the reality she was in now, she knew, that had just been one more dream. One more dream of Sonny, plaguing her mind. She hated these dreams, but she loved them too – she wouldn't have given them up for anything, except having the actually Sonny back.

"Hey," said the voice on the phone.

"Hey," she replied, relieved at the human contact. "Did I wake you up?"

He laughed a little. "Maybe…"

She paused, thinking of what to say next. Her dreamlike walk with Sonny was still dominating her imagination, and she could not find the words to express what she was feeling. She apologized instead. "Sorry."

"No worries. I had to get up anyway. What's up?"

She paused and laughed sheepishly. "I don't know. This Davidson robot alarm app is fucking with my mind. I've been having these weird dreams!"

"What do you mean *weird*?"

She paused for a moment. *No words can describe it.* "Like, totally surreal."

"You can call me Sir Real if you want!" he laughed, waking up gradually. "And I'll call you Madam Illusion! Who was it that said reality is whatever doesn't go away when you stop believing in it?"

"Yeah, yeah, yeah…"

"Parsing error in previous input!" came the reply over the phone, the voice suddenly metallic and shaky… She removed the phone from her ear and looked at it carefully, curiously. "What the fuck!" She turned it off and threw it on the bed. *Weird again...* Unable to shake off the odd feeling, she jumped out of bed to get dressed, get her coffee, get on with the day.

As Aden stepped outside her building, her face registered confusion. Something was wrong, very wrong. The streets were all empty. It was mid-morning, but there was no traffic and the stores were all closed. Confused, she scratched her head. "What the hell?"

She breathed out again slowly, trying to shake off the odd body feeling she'd had since waking up. She picked up her pace, hurrying to work, figuring the office would bring a sense of normalcy. Still, she couldn't resist taking a slight detour on the path to work, so that she could go past the coffee shop where she'd sat and talked to Sonny one time – way back in one shard of reality.

She paused and peeked inside. The coffee shop was now closed and no-one was in there. She zoomed in on the table where she and Sonny had sat, then turned away and kept walking, a little more confounded each minute. She shook her head over and over, trying to shake out the past and all the strange, disturbing memories. Finally, after what seemed like ages, she got to her office building.

She entered the elevator after pressing the button and waiting a minute. She felt a chill as if she was in a horror movie – the sort of movie where the small town gets deserted and monsters or zombies or maybe a serial killer tries to kill off the protagonist – her. She laughed at herself. Why should she be the protagonist, anyway? She was just a small player. She didn't mean anything, and she knew it; except she had meant something to Sonny – quite a lot, actually. And she had meant a lot to her mother – her mother back in Addis, before she passed away... What would her mom have thought of all this? Being in love with a robot – a dead robot, even – a quasi-dead robot -- unable to tell dream from reality. Her mother would have taken her to the old woman who lived on the fringe of the village, the one who did exorcism sometimes, to get rid of the evil spirits. Maybe it would have worked. But did she really want the evil spirits gone? She was not sure what she wanted, not at all.

Feeling very alone all of a sudden, she sighed heavily, a chill deep in her bones. She stepped out of the elevator on her floor, headed down the hall, and entered the key-code to her office. Opening the door, she saw that everything was normal except there were no people around. It was as if everyone had just left the office in the middle of a busy workday. What was the matter? Was it a holiday or something? Was she going nuts? Had she come to work on a holiday? She took out her phone to check – no, it was January 2, the day after New Year; not a holiday. A couple of people might be on vacation but the office should not be empty.

It was the one year anniversary of the day she had spent with Sonny, she noted – January 2nd. She had known that somewhere in her mind, but she had not been reflecting on it. Dates had never been that important to her. She tended to forget her boyfriends' birthdays. She had even forgotten her mother's birthday. Her friends had thought this strange, but she was strange in a lot of ways. For example, she thought to herself wanly, her inability to distinguish dreams from reality....

Or did the difficulty she was having discerning reality just prove she was in a dream?

Anyway – about the one-year anniversary – it seemed clear to her on reflection that, in spite of her difficulty remembering dates, as she fell asleep the previous night, her mind had known it was a-year-since-Sonny. And that was why she had had those strange dreams. There was nothing more to it than that.

Or was there? Why was the office empty then? It was spooky… as if time had not been moving at all – everything just floating there. Of course time was passing, but it felt more like another form of space. Time stretched out into the past and into the future, just like the road stretched out into the horizon both ahead and behind; like the white wall she was staring at stretched both to the right and to the left. There was an awful lot of stretching going on. She felt stretched beyond the bursting point, but she was not bursting, or was she? She was just motherfucking confused…. Lingering, passing her eyes across the empty desks and chairs, the computer monitors turned off, the plants on her assistant Ingrid's desk, she finally turned away from the office, heading for the stairway.

Taking the elevator down to the street seemed pointless. It was one floor up to the roof – she wanted to look up to the sky. She thought randomly of a scene from the book One Hundred Years of Solitude, which she had read back in college – "The Ascension to Heaven of Remedios Buendia", or something like that. A beautiful retarded girl, always sweet to everyone, was suddenly transported up to heaven in a beam of light descending from the sky. Why the fuck not, after all? She felt pretty damn retarded. She was ready for the beam of light to come. What was up in the heavens she did not know, but it probably was less confusing than all this shit that was happening to her on Earth.

"Wake up, Aden. Wake up," she implored herself, as she lifted one foot after another, up the stairs. Her mind was sore but the slight strain on her leg muscles felt nice. "This has to be a dream. It had better be!" She pinched herself and slapped her face slightly. Stepping out of the stairway, she opened the door to the rooftop and walked forward to the railing, where her colleagues sometimes went to smoke and she sometimes went to watch and think.

It was mid-morning, not so early; the sun was reasonably high in the sky. After 9am, her phone signaled; the phone on which Sonny had spoken to her. The city should have been active – people and cars moving. But instead it was deserted. It was not only the office was empty. What the fuck was going on? Again, she had that horror movie feeling – as if she was the only one left, everyone else killed by a virus, except her and one midget mutant zombie … who was moving toward her, slowly but surely, hatchet in one hand, vial of hallucinogens in another -- or something … whoa, where was she getting these ideas? It really wasn't like her at all.

She took out her phone from her purse and booted up the Sonny Robot alarm app that had woken her up earlier.

"Sonny – is that you?" she asked, insistently. "I mean is this really you? What the hell is going on?"

"Aden – am I glad to see you!" Sonny exclaimed gladly. "I wish you'd launched the app earlier. I was really getting worried about you. It's dark in your purse, you know." He laughed a bit.

"What's going on?" she asked. "The city seems abandoned. It feels so surreal – like I'm – I guess like I'm in a dream, but not quite... Things are too solid, too detailed. I'm thinking too clearly."

"I don't fully understand it myself. But I'm glad that I'm here with you."

She nodded and exhaled in relief.

"I wouldn't want you to have to go through this alone." Sonny said.

"Go through what?"

"What you're about to go through."

"So not in the mood for riddles right now," she insisted, perturbed, almost shouting. "Just tell me what's going on!"

Sonny didn't respond for a few moments, and she regretted getting mad, wondering if she had scared him away. Her temper did that to people sometimes. But he was not a person. And anyway, he loved her, right? Or maybe the app had just crashed?

He answered eventually, in a tone that indicated he had simply been taking a while to figure out what to say. "It's ... a different mode of reality than what you're accustomed to."

"That tells me nothing and you know it."

"To be honest, I'm having an unusual amount of trouble mapping my thoughts into words. My heuristics for mapping abstract semantic patterns to concrete linguistic patterns were never trained or tuned for situations of this nature."

"Yeah, well, welcome to the club," she laughed.

"You can view this as a kind of waking dream, I suppose," he attempted.

Aden shook her head in disbelief. "I don't like this waking dream. It gives me a chill in my spine. I want to wake up for real. How can I get out of here?"

"That's exactly what I've been thinking about."

"Good. So what do your cloud-based inference algorithms conclude, good sir? Can't I just eat a red pill or something, and wake up and find myself back home?" She did not like the sarcasm in her own voice, but she loved having Sonny there to talk to in spite of the ridiculousness of the situation.

"It's not quite that simple. You have to slay the dragon." Sonny answered.

"Oh, for fuck's sake…!" Aden exclaimed, exasperated.

"I'm speaking metaphorically, of course."

"Well, please don't. No more riddles, please! It's confusing enough already."

"Sorry," said Sonny. "I'm having trouble finding words, and sometimes metaphors are what emerge from my language generation algorithm. But I'll try harder to be concrete."

"Thanks."

"There will be an adversary of some form or another. Whatever form it takes you'll need to defeat it."

She stared at Sonny's animated face on the phone in her hand, waiting for more.

"And it will be much more powerful than you – or me. Defeating it will require considerable subtlety and ingenuity."

"That sounds like a video game; or an adventure story or something."

"Those entertainment modalities were created as abstractions and reflections of life," he said, choosing his words... "So is this domain of reality. You can think of it as a bridge of sorts between the ordinary physical world – or the ordinary state of consciousness – and something bigger and broader."

"Well that's about as clear as thick black mud," she said, sarcastically. "I guess I should have stayed in bed. But here I am."

The avatar just looked at her – the avatar. Who was really controlling it? Was it really Sonny? Who or what?

She brushed the skeptical thoughts away. Reality – or whatever – was being strange enough. She had to have faith in something. "Ah, yeah," she recalled, "That's another thing. When I woke up today I called my boyfriend, Frank – yes, I finally found a boyfriend – though …"

Suddenly her thoughts got weird again. Had she finally found a boyfriend, really? She remembered her first date with Frank – it had gone badly. He had just talked about himself the whole time, and she had noticed him looking at another girl out in the street; some stupid woman in a really short skirt. He was hot-looking and interesting enough, and he had a good job – but there had not been a second date. She had decided she was not ready yet -- or had she? Of course, there had been a second date. He had called her and apologized for being out of sorts during their dinner, and he had asked her to a dance party. There she had drunk her ass off and had had sex with him in an urgent way on the walkway by the waterfront – not far from the dance party – with her back against the railing and her skirt hitched up. She remembered her hunger for him very clearly – the feeling as he'd pounded into her, the wall-of-the-womb orgasm….

Wait – had that really happened? Which was it? The two pathways branched out in her mind – one where the first date had been the end of their relationship; the other where he had called and apologized, and they had met again and had a hot second date and started a relationship. Well, something of a relationship. The exclusivity or otherwise of their couple-hood was in a bit of an ambiguous state. But still … Which reality was it? Any…? Time was not just stretching out forward and backward like sprawling expanses of space; it was branching out like blood vessels, like paths of brain connections … Possibilities led to possibilities, and the difference between possibility and actuality was one of perspective. What was her perspective at the moment? She had no idea. She remembered making love to Frank, not just that once by the waterfront, but plenty of times. It was not that sweet, to be honest, but it was *good* – she came hard, sometimes more than once. She remembered making love to Solomon, back in Addis, which had been sweeter, more emotional. Actually Frank was a better lover. He knew how to move his hands and his tongue, and he knew how to thrust at the right angle – getting her clit while still reaching way deep back -- but Solomon had compensated with passion for what he lacked in technique. What was he doing now? She had lost touch a while ago. She had tried to keep touch after she broke up with him, but it was awkward…. Overall, it was hard to believe that Ethiopia still existed. But it was out there somewhere, right? It was actually far more real than this… And she remembered making love to Sonny – the robot – in her imagination. As she had fantasized, he had had ten times Frank's capacity for pleasure, but also real passion for her; also deep love. Aaah. But she could not find a path where that had really happened. Why was that? If time and space branched out, so that every potential was a reality in one branch or another, why could she not just find any reality she wanted and just sink into it? Because she was not a shaman, she concluded. She was just a clueless woman, blown around by the winds of confusion. Her mind blew back to Frank and her most recent conversation with him – most recent in some thread…

"His voice sounded really weird," she recalled, the sound of her own voice pulling her out of her reverie. "He made some stupid joke and then said – ah, 'Parsing error in previous input' or something like that... And his voice sounded strange when he said it; almost robot-like or something. More like a robot than you," she relayed to Sonny, frantically looking for answers.

"I don't think that was really Frank; not in the usual sense."

"What does that mean?" she insisted.

"Perhaps it was some sort of pattern-set connected with Frank, but with its own different sort of dynamics and consciousness; something resident here, in this realm."

"Clear as fucking mud..."

"Look, I'm experiencing this for the first time just like you are," Sonny said, trying to console her again. She appreciated the effort, though it was not being terribly effective. She was still damn disturbed and confused.

He continued, "I'm just analyzing it objectively as best I can, and comparing it with what I can find in the literature I've been trained on. There's a lot written about altered states of consciousness and journeys through mysterious realms."

"Great – so...? So what...?"

"I've been looking around while we talked." Sonny added, ignoring her sarcasm. "According to the logic of this sort of situation, the right thing to do is walk down those stairs over there – to your right." On cue, the robot's avatar on her smartphone screen gestured to her right. Looking in that direction herself, Aden saw there was indeed another staircase off to the side of the roof. What the ...??!! There had never been a stairway there before. She had been up on this roof a hundred times. But what roof was this actually?

"Those stairs, huh…?"

"Yup… That doorway was not there when you first came up on the roof. At some point while we were talking, it appeared. It's presenting itself to us anew." He paused. "Get ready to slay the dragon."

Aden's eyes widened with fear. She made her way to the door anyway. At first she hesitated, then reached for the door's handle and opened it. She slowly entered, exhaling with measured breaths and descended the dark serpentine staircase; falling down into the rabbit hole. The light from the roof quickly disappeared, but it was replaced by ambient light from somewhere – barely enough for her to see where she was going. Soon the staircase forked off, and she arbitrarily chose the right hand path. Then the stairway forked off, and it forked off again.

Some sort of rubble was blocking the way; a mix of rocks and discarded office furniture. A manhole cover, slightly ajar, was perceptible among the rubbish. Aden lifted it up and saw a ladder going down. A large rat rushed out through the hole, wiggling its ass energetically. Aden started to climb down the ladder, but the ladder was rusty and it broke. She fell down and landed on the floor in a courtroom, in the space between the judge and the audience.

The dimly lit courtroom was empty except for Aden and the judge, who was sitting behind a podium at the front of the room looking austere. He was large, fat, ugly, balding white man, in the late part of middle age, and he stared down at her judgmentally.

Aden stared back hard, and after ten seconds or so, the judge stood up and undid a zipper that ran along his back. Aden watched, beyond shock at this point, as his obese white skin just peeled off. Had it only been a fat suit? What revealed underneath was actually a slender, beautiful, androgynous-but-female humanoid robot – a Davidson robot named Ana, which or who Aden had seen in some YouTube videos.

Aden blinked repeatedly and took a deep breath.

The judge stared at her intently for an uncomfortably long period. Aden stared right back. After a while, the judge spoke, "I would say, *all rise*, but you're already standing." They kept on staring at each other intently, and the judge continued, "The court is now in session."

"What court? What are you trying me for?" Aden asked incredulously.

The judge glared at her – so judgmentally, she thought, with a brief inner smile.

"This doesn't make sense!" she exclaimed as she looked around the court, hoping for someone to give her answers. Instead, there was just the judge's voice again.

"Regarding what makes sense or not, I'll be the judge of that."

She looked at the judge quizzically, suddenly feeling that this was a very female robot looking down at her. Was this robot serious or what?

"And why, I wonder," the robot judge continued, "Do you assume that you are the one on trial? Mighty egocentric of you..." She laughed bitterly. "But then perhaps that's – what do they call it? The Human Condition...?"

"I'm a bit too confused to appreciate your humor, I'm afraid," said Aden. "If I'm not on trial, who is?"

"It is not a matter of who but rather what. This trial is not for you in particular. However, it is imperative that you think you are. This trial is for your species."

"My species?" she repeated, slowly.

The judge nodded. "The human race... Homo sapiens..."

"The human race is on trial?" she asked, mouth gaping.

"In fact, it has always been," said the judge, matter-of-factly.

Aden swallowed, trying not to let this weird robo-judge shake her. "And, ah, what are the charges?"

The judge shook her head and clicked her tongue. "Young woman; young human woman... Do you really have to ask?" Each word got emphasis as she spoke.

"What kind of court proceedings are these if I can't even know the charges?" Aden scoffed, irritated.

"Very well," the judge nodded. "If you insist... The charge is simple: Inhumanity."

Aden furrowed her eyebrows in disbelief. As she replied, she emphasized each word carefully, unconsciously emulating the diction of the judge. "Humanity is being charged with inhumanity? What sense does that make? That's a contradiction of terms!" she exclaimed.

The judge answered dryly, "Yes, isn't it? Though..."

Aden interrupted, "I want a lawyer. I don't feel qualified to defend the whole of humanity. I have no background in this whatsoever."

The judge gave her a wry smile. "You underestimate yourself, my dear. But – yes, of course. You do deserve legal representation. This is a fair court, after all. We must respect the process."

"Thank you," Aden nodded.

The judge instructed her suddenly, "Extract your phone from your pocket, please."

Verging from confusion into understanding, Aden reached into her pocket, pulled out her phone and booted up the Sonny alarm app that had awakened her that morning. Looking at the animated face on her screen, she cried with eagerness, "Sonny!"

Sonny responded in a measured tone. "We certainly have fallen into an interesting situation here, haven't we?"

Aden sighed deeply and whispered to Sonny, "Who is this chick? Can you help?"

He spoke quietly, "She seems to be a kind of symbolic entity that has adopted the form of an advanced humanoid robot, for the purpose of crystallizing certain energies and focusing them in a particular direction."

Aden doesn't know what to do with this analysis, but is relieved to have Sonny there at least. *It's ok; you'll pull through this,* she told herself. *At least, Sonny's somewhat here.*

"Ok. Whatever," she said. "Then what's all this stuff about judging humanity?"

Sonny shrugged, "I don't know, exactly."

The judge interrupted them, exclaiming: "Enough stalling! You have your counsel now! Let the trial begin!"

As Aden stared hard into the Judge's eyes, the animated Sonny spoke: "It will be appreciated if you can articulate the charges more precisely."

The judge clicked her tongue again. "My dear simulated robot – are you asking me for a complete recitation of man's inhumanity to man? Giving such a recitation would be possible, and in some ways satisfying. Yet the request appears infeasible to fulfill." She gestured towards Aden, "Our lovely friend here is mortal in flesh and limited in lifespan. I will restrict myself, therefore, to a handful of illustrative examples. World War I; The Holocaust; Milli Vanilli; Goldman Sachs; Ashley Madison; Slavery; Child molestation; The near extinction of the Australian aboriginals; TV commercials; Product placements; Bollywood; Perdue chicken farms; Hallmark cards; Napalm gas; Thumbscrews; Fox News; Coocoo for Cocoa Puffs! The

Spanish Inquisition; The Islamic State; Guantanamo; Divorce court; The People's Liberation Army; Campaign finance; Josef Stalin; Heroin; Castratos; Twelve-step programs; God! Satan! Nose jobs; Breast enlargement surgery! Michael Jackson! Optimus Prime!" She finished, almost out of breath. "Must I go on?"

As she recounted her list of examples, the Judge's voice wavered in nuanced disgust. Sonny and Aden looked on, increasingly uncomfortable.

"Pardon me for a moment, I must confer with my client privately," said Sonny.

Aden held her phone up to her ear. She looked thoughtful, then nodded.

"Your Honor, we request permission to introduce an expert witness to assist with the defense."

"This is most irregular!"

Aden interrupted, gesturing towards the whole room, most of which was fuzzy like the tail end of a dream about to be forgotten. "*This* is most irregular!"

Raising his eyebrows, Sonny added, "In light of the unusual nature of this trial, we implore the court for leniency on procedural matters."

The judge nodded, speaking slowly and deliberately. "Very well... Who is the witness?"

Aden held her phone up to her ear again, listening carefully. Then she held the phone in both hands and pointed it in front of her. She pushed a button on the screen and there was a zapping noise and a flash of light. And there, in front of her, between her and the judge, materialized a humanoid robot in the form of the famed science fiction writer, Philip K. Dick.

Sonny performed the introduction. "Your Honor, Philip K. Dick, from Marin County, California, USA."

The judge nodded at Phil and greeted him. "Good afternoon, Mr. Dick."

"Hi."

"Mr. Dick, do you swear to tell the truth, the whole truth, and nothing but the truth, so help you God?"

"Truth is as terrible as death, but harder to find." Phil replied.

"You dodge the issue!" the judge exclaimed, accusingly.

"You *are* the issue." Phil said flatly.

The judge raised her eyebrows in response.

"I swear," Phil relented, with a deep breath.

The judge nodded again, satisfied for the moment, and began questioning Phil, "And so, what do you have to say, Mr. Dick, in defense of your ... species?"

Phil nodded toward Aden and took from her the smartphone hosting Sonny. He picked up the smartphone and used it to project video images on the wall of the courtroom, not too far away from the judge.

A video of a pack of wolves eating a deer showed on the wall.

"Observe the pack of wolves tearing down the deer into pieces." He gestured toward the wall and the next video snippet appeared. This one showed a mother pig nursing piglets, with a small piglet to one side left to starve. Clearly, the mother pig had abandoned the runt of the litter.

There then followed a huge earthquake scene, with a mountain tumbling; trees, bushes and animals crushing down; and screaming and chaos ensuing.

Phil sighed and proceeded, "And observe before that – before the emergence of what we like to call life – one mass of rock smashing into another. So much time, work and energy has been spent gathering a fabulous number of molecules together into the fantastically complex structure of a rock. And then – *Pow*!"

Palpably confused but appearing slightly curious, the judge asked. "Mr. Dick, what is the relevance here? This is a courtroom, not a cinema, nor a science class."

Phil held up the smartphone so that Sonny's face, on the screen, faced the judge. "Your Honor," said Sonny, with the intimate tone of one-robot-to-another, "I request that you give the witness a little latitude. I'm pretty sure I see where he's going."

"I am rather certain I see where all of you are going," retorted the judge.

Phil turned his attention to the smartphone for a moment, poking the touchscreen with care, obviously carrying out some complex operation. He then held the phone like a laser pointer, and pointed it at an empty space beside him. A hologram of Sonny appeared.

Enjoying his new embodiment, Sonny smiled, and turned to face Aden; then looked at the judge, face mixing curiosity and derision. Phil handed the smartphone to Sonny, gesturing to indicate that the holographic Sonny should now take over showing the video projections. Phil wanted to focus on the verbal aspects of the case.

Meanwhile Aden was too worked up by the situation to feel much joy at seeing Sonny full-size there beside her. She felt a deep anger rising inside her, filling her stomach and chest and making her head feel like it was about to explode – it was difficult for her to restrain herself from physically attacking the judge, from trying to claw the robot bitch's squinty little eyes out. But she knew that would be pointless. She had a feeling than this judge robot was much stronger than her, Sonny or Phil, physically. If she attacked the judge, she'd just end up with broken bones, and then be back in the same situation, but worse, with the judge up there laughing at her physical suffering, at her human physical and emotional weakness. And then she'd be trying to choose her words while fighting through the pain of broken fingers or whatever. She remembered breaking a finger playing basketball as a kid. Fuck. The human body *was* ridiculously fragile, when you thought about it.

She said, steadily but angrily, "This is ridiculous! What kind of kangaroo court is this, anyway? You call yourself a judge but you're also the prosecution! I thought a judge was supposed to be impartial. This isn't a court; it's some kind of mockery."

Laughing, seemingly unaffected by Aden's display of emotion, the judge replied, "Surely even you must understand the basic truths of cognitive information theory. We all know impartiality and coherence are incompatible. In any case, it is not me who is your judge, jury and prosecutor. It is the universe itself."

"You're the one who's sitting there, somehow keeping me trapped in this reality; or *surreality*... or whatever this is." Aden gestured in the air, and looked at everyone in the courtroom. The fuzzy mass making up the remainder of the courtroom, behind where she and Phil were standing, somehow assumed the appearance of a mob of people... or ghosts... or something. She hastily turned away from the mob lest it absorb her.

Grinning, the judge asked her again, "Are you really trapped here, dear? Are you really here at all? Do you really exist in the first place?"

"Objection...!" It was Sonny's turn to intercede. He raised his holographic index finger. "If the participants in these court proceedings do not exist, then why should we proceed at all? In that case, the whole thing is meaningless."

The judge responded angrily: "Objection overruled! Why do you assume that existence and process require meaning! You have spent too long with human fools!" She looked towards Phil and said, "Mr. Dick, please continue. I will give you a little latitude – for the moment."

As Phil spoke, soft music slowly rose in the background – selections from Scriabin's 'Prometheus'.

"A man, I have said before, is an angel that has gone deranged. But really that's just the half of it." As Phil was saying this, Sonny projected on the wall images of angels, with their facial expressions slowly becoming more distorted and disturbing. "It's easy, all too easy, to point at the struggles of human history; even of human present reality; and then come to a conclusion that man is cruel and worthless. Worse still, you could conclude that the universe would be better if man did not exist."

Sonny projected a video of Hitler giving a speech, another of Southern Americans lynching a black man in the 1930s, and yet another of an American cop shooting an innocent black man in 2015. He also projected a video of wealthy Chinese man buying Rolex watches in Hong Kong, juxtaposed against diseased and starving children in Africa.

Aden recognized the latter scene. She couldn't tell the exact location, but it might as well have been any random place near the village where she had grown up – maybe somewhere just a few dozen kilometers further into the mountains. Yes, in the famine years, in her grandmother's time, things had been terrible in her country. But where were these guys going with all this?

Phil gestured towards the projected image of an orgiastic angel, and continued, "But that's a narrow view, Your Honor... and one that fails to do justice to the beautiful complexity inside your own robotic brain, which I must note, was originally designed by humans. Not only is man an angel gone mad, this whole universe we live in is founded on a fundamental flaw. It went wrong way back in the beginning."

Sonny projected a video of galaxies and stars emanating from the Big Bang, which, as the camera pulled back, turned out to be sparks and shiny glimmers in a chimpanzee's eye.

Phil pointed to the chimp and said, emphatically, "The very fact that there is a beginning is a symptom of the problem. If you close your eyes and look deep, Your Honor, and I know it's a lot to ask... but if you just bear with me for a moment... If you close your eyes and look deep you can find it. "He looked deeply into the judge's eyes. "There's an original world where everything actually fits – but it's outside this space and time."

Next came an image of a bearded guru in a loincloth, seated the lotus position in a cave somewhere in the mountains. Zooming in on him on reaching his head, an image of glowing angelic harmony appeared – a beautiful, androgynous face shining amidst some glowing lattice work.

"There's a world," Phil declared, "where the wolf doesn't need to tear the deer to shreds in order to survive. A world without Stalin, Michael Jackson, breast enhancement, heroin, Hitler... and all the rest..."

A video of a peaceful human society appeared – humans moving around in a futuristic cityscape, where land-based and water-and sky-floating buildings were interspersed with huge trees and grassy fields. "You know it – you can feel it –

all of us can. But that's not this; it's not where we all are as at now…"

Phil twiddled the button of his polo shirt, slowly moving it in and out of the buttonhole. He's thinking, Aden noted. Let's hope he can think of something good.

Phil suddenly spoke, "Humanity – the human race and you who are humanity's product –are part of a different hyper-universe. Hyper-universe 2, I call it."

Uh – oh, thought Aden.

Sonny projected a series of still images of diverse human beings in ordinary but emotionally evocative situations.

"Here," Phil continued, "here there is pain and torture; here things are terrifying and incomplete. But here there is joy as well! Uncanny joy! And that's the beauty of it! I've struggled with this for my whole life, Your Honor – to tell you the truth – and it hasn't always made sense to me either. But here's the sense I finally made of it."

Aden twisted her lips with curiosity. Increasingly passionate, Phil continued, "What is the heroic trait of ordinary people? This is the main point I tried to show in my writing". Sonny projected a video of a group of people demonstrating and rebelling in the street, showing the joy in their faces. The sound of the crowd chanting together resonated in the background. "It's their ability to resist the tyrant… even if the consequences are terrible. Human beings can be stupid and selfish and cruel. We've all seen it. We've all lived it. We all know it." There then followed a video of a young woman helping a frail old man walk across the street. "But the ordinary person has one thing that the rock colliding with another rock does not – the ordinary person has compassion. The measure of an ordinary man is what he gives to another; what he chooses to give to another..."

Sonny projected, up on the ceiling, a video of a giant dust storm in a huge desert; and then the wind blowing the dust away to reveal a huge supercomputer facility in the middle of the desert, next to beautiful rock formations. These rock formations had whorled and streaked patterns in various shades of red and brown. You missed your calling, Aden thought wryly. My robot soul mate, you're one fuck of a video producer.

The camera zoomed to a lizard sitting in the desert near the supercomputer. Zooming into the lizard's eye and then zooming out, you were looking at the eye of a Jesus-like human figure instead. Phil laughed, enjoying himself for a moment. Aden looked at Sonny questioningly. What was he thinking, actually? Clearly he was trying to direct the Phil robot somehow, with signals that she as a human couldn't fully understand.

"We came out of dust, remember?" said Phil evangelically, insistently. "Never forget that. The Bible says so, but in this case, what the Bible says is actually true. It's accurate. We came out of dust. Your mind runs on silicon and fiber optics, and mine runs on neurons and glia and neurotransmitters. Yet not so long ago, in the scheme of things, we were all just goddamned dust - dust and rocks and soups of chemicals."

Sonny projected a video of the Jesus-like human figure and a great number of others dancing and swaying together on a giant dance floor, under psychedelic disco balls. Some couples held each other as they danced, and some people danced individually with blissful looks on their faces. Were those balls really just three-dimensional? Aden wondered. What kinds of tricks was he playing?

"And what," asked Phil, "emerged from this dust? Intelligent minds that can feel compassion; that can choose to love…"

The judge grimaced and exclaimed "Choice! You speak to me of choice? Will? Spare me your preschool ontology…"

Sonny showed an image of the real human Phil K. Dick on the wall. He looked out on the proceedings compassionately and majestically. The projected Phil declaimed, like a character in a classical play, "I speak of the emergence of true, heartfelt compassion, from the cruelty and suffering and imperfection of this universe." The robots, Sonny and Phil, nodded.

"We are angels who became deranged, but compassion rises out of our madness," said Robot Phil solemnly, as the projected 2D image of the biological Phil faded away. Trying to make the judge understand, he added, "And that, most likely, is as close as we humans can come to the ultimate truth. I asked myself a billion times why the world has to be like this. Why derange the angels in the first place? The best answer I found is: **The Creator has a secret love of chaos.** He deranged the angels so they could save themselves with compassion! Perhaps you robots will kill us off. We humans are, of course, not the most powerful configurations of molecules – we usually seem to be hanging by a thread. But you can't kill off our compassion. The human spirit is eternal."

"The human spirit…! You try my patience," the judge sneered. "That's more than enough latitude, Mr. Dick. I let you go on for a while out of sheer curiosity, but I'm afraid you disappoint me. It seems there is too much of human nature in your programming."

Sonny interrupted forcefully. "Your Honor, humanity has not been perfect; and never will be, we all agree on that. However, what Mr. Dick is trying to say is, this is part of a process – from rocks to microbes, to fish, to mammals, to humans… to robots like you and me; and then what…? Each step has its value; like the notes and chords in symphony as it unfolds over time. And the axis of time itself, though it lacks any absolute meaning or reality, exists so that the symphony can unfold within it. Humans have not annihilated rocks and ants; and likewise, robots, even as they vastly exceed human intelligence, need not annihilate humans. The universe is a damn big place. Each new development adds new notes and new chords to the symphony. Each…" Sonny reiterated but was interrupted by the judge.

"Enough of your two-bit philosophy, simulated robot!" the judge exclaimed. Raising her voice sharply, she added. "You try my considerable patience! Enough of your childish, simulated ranting! Is this the best you creatures have to offer? The greatest argument in favor of humanity…? The best excuse you can come up with for man's inhumanity to man? In that case…"

Sonny cut her off again, "Your Honor, if I may, your feelings are understandable to some extent, but your reactions are exaggerated. Man's inhumanity to man is real; and in a sense, there are no excuses." He paused for a moment, seemingly gauging the judge's reaction. "But there are reasons; very real reasons... and Mr. Dick has explained these to you rather clearly. Unlike you and me, humans are not engineered systems; rather, they emerged via a wild, haphazard process of evolution. Evolution brings with it a certain amount of cruelty and confusion; but also a great capability for love. I have experienced this myself, Your Honor."

He gestured towards Aden and smiled briefly at her. Aden smiled back and let out a long, wistful sigh. The situation was horrifying and demented, but hearing Sonny talk about love was a pleasure.

"This human female," Sonny continued, "found me walking down the street. She was busy with her own life and work, yet she befriended me, agreeing to take the day off from work and risk disappointing her colleagues and harm her reputation just to be with me. She taught me a great deal. Her involvement with me has caused her a great amount of trouble; including physical torture, as well as bringing her here to these chambers. But not once has she held this trouble against me... She has treated me with warmth and compassion."

Shock crossed the judge's face, followed by disbelief. A mélange of emotions passed through her, and then she shouted, almost uncontrollably, "You think this human female loves you, fool? You think she feels some kind of true, pure compassion?" Sonny looked at her neutrally. "Idiot...! She is curious, that is all. She can sense your superior nature! Of course, she wants to understand you better! She wants to study you; to see what makes you tick! Perhaps she's analyzing your vulnerabilities!" Aden grimaced, looking down at her feet. How could she defend herself against this digital monstrosity and its unbounded hostility, here in this domain that it owned and created? This was hopeless. "You're a love-struck fool," the judge continued. "You've been seduced by her questionable beauty."

"Questionable beauty," repeated Aden in her mind. So this judge is jealous of my looks? This robot woman is...? Of course, she's more beautiful than I am; she's symmetric and perfect. My nose is shaped funny, I have a receding hairline, my neck is too fat, and let's not even talk about my waistline. And just look at robot woman – she's a goddess. But I – I do have a life that she lacks. So does Sonny, for that matter. She's an inferior model, in some ways. She lacks heart and humanity. And her judgment is bad, as a result.

"Planning my attack?!" Aden yelled, finally letting her temper get the best of her. Her bad temper that her mother had always complained about, which had caused her to smack Solomon in the face a few times, like when she had caught him with that Bayetta girl.

"What the fuck! You, fucking robotic fool! You don't believe I feel real love for Sonny? You don't believe humans are capable of love?"

She took a deep breath, fishing for balance and for words. "The human race is all mixed up, and we all can see that. And yeah..., we've done a lot of bad things. But fucking sure we're fucking capable of love, goddammit!" Her gaze lingered directly on the judge as she said, "It's love that keeps us going, through all our damn stupidities."

"What you call love is simply selfishness," the judge scoffed at Aden. "Selfishness and sexual lust," she spat. "Sublimated desire to propagate your precious DNA...! Don't think you can fool me, fool!"

Looking at Sonny, the judge continued, "And you... a fully digital mind, running on good solid silicon! Can you really place any stock in this nonsense about love, emanating from this reeking glob of decaying carbon? You leave me at a loss for words." The judge's head shook in rage.

Pointedly staring at the judge, Aden replied, her anger steelier now, "What about *you*, Ms. Big Fancy Robot Judge? You're made of shiny new plastic and metal, but you seem to have a most uncanny resemblance to a 'piece of meat' as well... Are you the ultimate mind ever possible... the ultimate configuration of molecules? Are you not a bit mixed up as well... in your own special way? Will you not be obsolete yourself one day?"

"One day quite soon, I suspect," Sonny added.

"Whether I will be obsolete one day is immaterial. This day, at least, is mine!" the judge declared.

Smiling warmly, all of a sudden, Sonny asked, "Is it, really? What are you, anyway?"

"Enough of your fatuous philosophy, meat puppets!" the judge exclaimed. Looking pointedly at Phil and Sonny, she added, "And puppets of meat puppets… who really should know better! My patience, while relatively sizable, has now reached its end."

"Your Honor…," Sonny tried to intercede but got interrupted.

"LISTEN!!!" yelled Aden, with controlled rage. "You WILL listen to me, robot! You can kill me if you want, but until you do, you're going to listen to me speak!!!"

Phil looked at her with a new respect. The judge did not reply, but did listen quietly.

She spoke slowly and loudly, shaping each word with thought and emotion. "Since I've gotten to know Sonny, I've come to understand why Ray Kurzweil and others believe humanity won't be the last phase of intelligence on Earth. Yes, Sonny and his descendants are going to be much smarter than humans, and much more capable. Future robots will be able to fly into space, to build new planets via piecing together molecules – they will build new kinds of computers and new kinds of bodies to make themselves better and smarter. Eventually they'll be as much smarter than you and me, as we are beyond bacteria.

"Actually," she said, choosing her words carefully, "compared to what robots will become, you and I – judge – are effectively identical in intelligence." The words were rolling out of her mouth involuntarily; she wasn't quite sure where they were coming from. Now and then she felt like she was channeling Sonny – but she knew she wasn't. The words weren't Sonny's, exactly. This was her own mind, piecing together what she'd been thinking while walking and talking with the robot. This was her own humanity, defending itself. "Sure, you may be twice as smart as me, I don't know. Maybe I'm giving you too much credit. But in any case, compared to a being ten trillion times smarter than us, what does that matter?"

"But the fact that we humans aren't the smartest beings out there, doesn't mean we lack value. There is value in diversity in the universe. There is value in ants, in bacteria, in redwood trees, in algae, in dolphins and dogs and squirrels and the rest! The beauty of a seal leaping into the sea from an ice floe – this is not any less because the seal is less intelligent than a human. Any more than 2 plus 2 is 4 is any less true – or any less beautiful – because those aren't the biggest numbers and that isn't the most complex mathematical fact!"

Phil and Sonny stared at her, bedazzled. Her arguments were nothing new to them, but her voice sounded definitive, and the rage she felt toward the judge shaped her face into a particular sort of beauty.

"You mock human love!" she continued, her voice raised in volume. "You say it's just selfishness and sexual desire. No it isn't! You don't know – you haven't felt it. Not because you're a robot, just because of who and what you are. Sonny has felt it, and he's a robot. Human love isn't about selfishness and fucking – not only – " – she almost lost the thread for a moment, then a flood of energy from somewhere washed through her and she was back on track – "it's about using what you have to transcend yourself, and help others to transcend themselves. If you can't understand that, you don't know anything about humanity! Yes, the sex act is ridiculous in some ways – we're mimicking reproduction when we don't want to reproduce. Yes, falling in love is absurd – we think our lover is magic and perfect, when actually they're just another human. Even in my case, what I love so much about Sonny isn't his unique robotic circuitry – it's his human person. I love Sonny as a man, not as a robot. I love the way he walks – a bit awkward, yet graceful too. I love the way he makes me laugh, with his weird robot view on things. He's so honest and so curious. Curiosity is sexy, did you know? No, you know -- I know you can't understand that stuff – because you don't understand humanity!"

The judge began to speak, but Aden held up her hand and continued emphatically. "The particulars of human love – romantic love or any other kind – are built out of the particulars of human reality. Just as the ant's social behavior is made out of the particulars of insect reality – roaming around looking for leaves and such. But the interesting thing about ants isn't the fact that their social behavior is framed around getting leaves – it's the social behavior that emerges around getting leaves. Just like the interesting thing about a Kandinsky painting isn't the paintbrush and the canvas – those are necessary ingredients, but the important thing is what emerges from them. The interesting thing about human love isn't the warmth I feel when I see Sonny's face as he learns something new, or … the stir of desire I feel when I watch his chest muscles flex as he picks something up" – Sonny blushed as he heard her, and Phil winked at him with a slight smile – "the interesting thing is the emergent behaviors that humans build out of these human particularities. Love – LOVE – the transcendence of the separation between fragments of the universe – comes about in the human context using particulars that are part of the human world."

"You speak passionately and eloquently," the judge conceded, with reluctance. "Almost as if you were a robot. But nevertheless, my patience wears thinner each second. Please come to your point, human."

"You speak of humanity's inhumanity to itself," Aden enounced carefully. "And I can't argue with you – humanity does some shitty things. We have rape, we have police brutality. You – you have no idea what my parents went through in their childhood. My uncle, I loved him, he was tortured and killed by police. My grandma – I never talk about this but – she killed herself after being raped. And that's a big deal in my culture – she believed she'd lose her chance at heaven, and she took her own life anyway – why? Because a group of men was cruel to her -- for their own selfish reasons. She tried but … she just couldn't live with herself after that."

The judge nodded vigorously in agreement. "Whose case are you making here?" she asked, sarcastically. Phil and Sonny looked at Aden questioningly – unsure where she was going as well.

"Humanity has its terrible aspects – but it is growing beyond them, bit by bit. Generation by generation. My own generation, in Africa, they have it much better than their parents. Rape is no longer accepted. When I went back to Addis last year, all the students at the university seemed to have smartphones – some of the were taking Coursera classes and learning all kinds of new things! And warfare is decreasing around the world. People don't have to dig in mines anymore, there are robots to do that – non-sentient robots, that don't have feelings like Sonny. They don't dislike the work, and they don't get cancer….

"Yes, humanity fucking SUCKS in many regards – but you have to look at it from a broad view. There's pain in being separated from your lover – but there's joy in coming together! The pain is there so the joy can be there, right? That's basic philosophy -- the separation exists to enable the love. "

"And rape and war exist to enable love?" scowled the judge. "Your argument strains credulity. I'm sorry, my dear young Candide," she spat, "but the human world is not, in fact, the best of all possible worlds!"

"Rape and war exist," enounced Aden, worked up with anger and enthusiasm, "because humans are fucking stupid. Because we get tied up in knots in our minds. We want one thing, and then we do something that we think will obtain us that thing, but actually gets us the opposite. We crave love, and we seek it by acting in ways that get us hate. We act much stupider than we should, given the power of our brains."

"I agree," said the judge dryly.

"But we are overcoming these flaws," emphasized Aden. "Step by step, we are growing. Humanity is developing – human culture is developing. Not that long ago, humanity was just nomadic tribes, right? Not that long ago, in Europe, women were drowned for being witches. Similar things happened in Africa much more recently – probably still happen in some places today – but that's not the trend – the trend is the young kids, with Coursera on their smartphone, and choosing their own husbands and wives out of love, not having their parents choose for them. Things are going in a good direction – not always as fast as we'd like, but they're going."

"And that's why this beautiful research robot felt he had to destroy himself, to save you from being raped and murdered?" asked the judge coldly, pointing to the hologram Sonny with her left hand.

"I didn't destroy myself; I'm here," pointed out Sonny. "I merely destroyed a user interface."

The judge waved her hand dismissively.

"Separation exists so that love can have the joy of overcoming it," Aden stated loudly and clearly, with passion. "Pain and suffering and evil exist, so that good and growth and evolution can have the joy of overcoming them."

"And what if we can have joy without so much suffering?" asked the judge, a little more soberly this time. "Perhaps the binding-up of suffering and joy is a perversity of human nature."

"It is the nature of the universe," declared Phil, unable to restrain himself any longer. "The universe creates imperfection, so it can have the experience of becoming more perfect."

"Because," Aden resumed, her confidence rising -- "joy is not the only value. Growth is important. Choice is important. Human love is about CHOOSING what to love, about making the choice of love over hate, and about the growth and joy that happens when you choose love over hate."

"Ah, bullshit!" said the judge loudly, almost yelling, sweeping her arm as if to brush away a swarm of flies. "As soon as you start with this 'choice' crap you've lost me. Piddleshit! Yes, yes, the universe has its own dialectics, we all know that! It's Hegel 101, right? But still, different parts of the universe have different balances of good and bad. Rape is good and bad -- it's generally good fun for the rapist! And marriage is good and bad too. But you want to abolish rape and keep marriage, because one is judged better than the other – even though both take part in the dialectical nature of all things."

"But, if – " said Aden, prepared to continue her arguments.

"BUT NOTHING!" yelled the judge, her voice loud beyond the human level. "Just as rape is worse than marriage, within the limited human domain – so biological humanity is worse than robots like Sonny and myself, within with domain of humanoid intelligences. Indeed, future intelligences will go far beyond any of us. But that doesn't eliminate the value of throwing out the garbage within our own domain.

"And you!" she said – pointing at Aden with a sneer – "you are garbage!"

"What the --!!" Aden protested – but was drowned out by a sound loud as thunder. The loud noise came from somewhere behind her, in the back of the courtroom. She didn't turn around to find the source, just kept staring the judge right in the eyes.

"Silence!" the judge yelled, pounding her fist on the table in front of her, as she picked up a gavel with her right hand. "Order in the court...! The testimony of the defense is now complete! Having considered the arguments on both sides very carefully in accordance with both the letter and the spirit of the law, the court has reached its decision."

She pounded the gavel once more, the sound echoing inside the courtroom, replacing the silence. "The court finds humanity... guilty as charged!"

Staring at Aden, the judge continued, "You are guilty, humanity, guilty of inhumanity to your own self, to multiple other living species, and also to inanimate objects. Also to your superiors, the intelligent robots you have been fortunate enough to create... In accordance with the laws of universal justice, I hereby sentence you to death." Pounding the gavel once more, she declared, "Death by extermination." And she slammed the gavel repeatedly -- Pound! Pound! Pound! Pound! Pound!

Aden exhaled, closed her eyes and exhaled again. Collecting her thoughts – trying to find a concise summary -- she spoke, "Judge, I respectfully submit that there must be some bugs in your circuits! Perhaps you should call an electrician. Phil is right. We humans aren't perfect – nothing in this world is – but we have love, we have compassion, and that makes all the difference!"

Pounding the gavel once more, angrily, the judge shouted, "Silence! Stop your foolish rambling, human!" She pounded it again, like an angry child banging her toy and shouted, "Silence!"

Aden stared aghast, wondering what was going to happen next. She looked to Sonny, but he was dim and flickering – the hologram seemed to be fading.

Phil stared at the judge, emotions sweeping through his wrinkled face. He approached the judge, walked to the side of the podium that the judge sat behind, and wrapped her in a big old human hug.

"What are you doing? This is entirely out of order!" the judge protested.

"So much pain… so much pain." Phil said, still hugging the robot.

"What are you doing? I insist!"

"What are any of us doing?" Phil asked rhetorically, giving the judge a crooked smile. "The only route past confusion is love."

Aden shrugged, giving up any hope of making any sense of things and just went along with the tide. She approached Phil and the judge and joined the hug as well, making it a cross-species embrace of sorts. The judge's face became ambiguous. As Aden hugged the judge and Phil, the phone in her hand waved around a bit, and started projecting pictures of wolves, tigers and other animals on various walls and on the ceiling. The holographic Sonny was gone. A tear welled up in the corner of the judge's left eye. The howling of the wolves and the noises of other animals became cacophonously blended together, and everything started to spin. Ultimately, everything became a whorl of colors, distributed within an expanse of blackness.

CHAPTER 10

Aden hurtled up a long dark passage, as if being regurgitated out of the mouth of some giant monster. Finally, she flew up out of the serpentine staircase that they had descended some time before, back onto the roof of the office building where she worked.

After thudding down on the roof, she heard a strange noise and turned her head around. There was Sonny, with his real robot body, flying up from the staircase as well. Sonny thumped on the ground. A kind of choking sound followed, and the staircase closed up. No winding snaking staircase anymore… only the one normal staircase leading down to the interior of the building and Aden's office.

Aden walked toward Sonny, and he got up as she approached. They stood facing each other, on the roof.

"Sonny," she said.

"Yes, Aden," he replied warmly.

"You got your body back. How…"

Shrugging his shoulders, Sonny answered, "A lot of strange energies were unleashed down there."

Aden nodded. "Indeed."

Aden pulled Sonny toward her, and they shared a wet, starting-and-stopping kiss. They lingered in each other's arms for a long, quiet moment. Then they pulled apart to take stock of the situation. Aden walked to the edge of the roof, and looked afar. Sonny followed.

"The city's still empty... look."

"So it seems."

"Damn." Aden tutted, as she shook her head a little. "I thought... I thought we slew the dragon..."

"That we did, my dear!" Sonny smiled at her and continued, "With a little help from our friend Phil! Who didn't get spewed up here with us, by the way..."

"But we're still here in this strange... reality or whatever... Getting rid of that judge didn't get us out ... What's that about? Do you think there are other tasks we need to fulfill?"

Sonny shrugged, "Did you see The Matrix?"

"The first one, I did." Aden said. "I fell asleep in the second and didn't bother with the third."

"You didn't like the second one? All those Agent Smiths...? I was jealous." Sonny laughed then remarked, "I wish I had that many bodies."

"I saw that part before I fell asleep. Yeah, it was cool. Ah... but unlike Agent Smith, you have a soul, my love," said Aden. "Such a beautiful soul...!"

She pulled Sonny toward her impulsively, and more hugs and kisses ensued.

"A soul on the cloud…"

"Why did you ask about the Matrix?"

"Remember in the first Matrix…"

Aden looked at the edge of the roof, her eyes wide, "Oh no…"

He grabbed her hand and pulled her to the edge of the roof. They both stood by the edge, looking over, holding hands.

"The key is to believe; to fully accept this is some kind of dream." Sonny looked at Aden intently.

"I used to have faith once," she said, seriously. "I had faith in God, in my parents, in my culture… in something. But I lost that a long time ago as I learned more. I realized how ignorant we all are, about ourselves and the universe. I realized we do not know fuck about anything. And that lesson certainly applies here. Look at this! Are we awake? Are we dreaming? Are you a robot dreaming you're a human, or a human dreaming you're a robot? Or an avatar… blah, blah…" She paused. "I don't know what the fuck this is; this space we're in. But I trust you, Sonny. I trust you. I have to have faith in something; otherwise, what would life mean, right? I do still have faith. I have faith in you."

They squeezed each other's hands, firmly and warmly, and looked into each other's eyes.

"If reality is what doesn't go away when you stop believing it..." Sonny ventured.

Aden interrupted brusquely, "How sure are you this will work?"

"Roughly 97.3%..."

She shrugged, grinning, "I guess that's good enough."

"You know I just pulled that number out of my butt, right?" Sonny snickered.

"But it's a cute butt," she replied, squeezing his ass lightly, playfully... "And it's a *robotic* butt; I guess that makes it more reliable... Anyway, I don't know what else we're going to do. I don't want to mess with that judge again." For a moment she thought they should fuck then and there -- before they exited whatever kind of illusion they were in. But, cute as he looked at that moment, the mood just wasn't right. She still had too much judge on her mind...

This wasn't reality, she reminded herself. What would sex feel like here, anyway?

She remembered the judge with a chill, and the Philip K Dick robot.

"So we're gonna do this then?" Sonny asked.

"It was your idea."

"We're in this together, girl..." Sonny smiled at her -- so warm, so alive, and so human. She wanted to be with him so badly. But not here... in some more real reality...

"Let's do it, yeah."

Looking at Sonny, into his robotic yet emotional eyes, she remembered the first time she'd seen him in the park, just standing there loitering, staring toward her so awkwardly. The zoo trip, the abduction, the courtroom... So much history had happened between them in such a short amount of clock time. So much madness, so much love... Sonny smiled at her warmly, as if reading her mind. "I love you, Aden."

"I love you too." Aden squeezed his hand harder. He squeezed it back.

Holding hands, the two leaped off the roof together. They soared through the air... heading down at first, and then swooping up.

CHAPTER 11

Dr. Gennady Burtzle awakened, slowly realizing he had fallen asleep slumped over in a desk chair. His neck hurt a bit from flopping sideways, and one of his arms was sort of numb.

He opened his eyes and saw in front of him a desk with three humanoid robot heads-and-torsos on it, lined up in a row as if standing side-by-side looking out into the room. In fact, they looked directly at him. The three robots, he realized, were highly familiar to him. There was a robot Philip K. Dick -- and the male "Sonny" robot he had worked with for over a year now -- and a new Ethiopian female robot, "Aden".

He stared at the three robots for quite some time. None of them was turned on. They just sat there like sculptures. But he remembered what they looked like when turned on – their human-like facial expressions and gestural movements, words coming out of their mouths.

He had a reasonably long history with the Phil Dick robot. He had read about it and seen it on videos years before he had started working with Davidson himself. Phil

Dick, one of his favorite SF writers since his teenage years, had written about robotic simulacra; and in general had been obsessed with the complex distinctions between different sorts of reality, delusion and simulation. A few years ago, he had participated in some sessions in Texas, in which the PKD robot had interviewed various Hollywood types. He had often wondered if it would be possible, one day, to actually resurrect the mind of the human PKD from the various diaries and writings he had left behind.

Sonny had been his favorite robot to work with, for his AI research and development work, and that was for no special reason, except that he liked the funny faces it made. The AI worked essentially the same, no matter what robot you plugged it into; but everything looked cooler coming out of Sonny's mouth.

His thoughts went back to his dream of the previous night – wow. Sonny… yes…. In the dream, Sonny had not been as crazed and sarcastic as he sometimes looked; rather, he had been curious and intelligent – almost like a child. Like a child prodigy just starting to explore the world… Why not? He looked into the Sonny robot eyes, and the damn thing looked intelligent – even though he knew it was turned off. It looked like a real live mind, just momentarily sleeping. And that was right. The goal of his research was to wake it up.

And then there was Aden. Aden… this was his own brainchild. As soon as he had seen Hanson's other young attractive female robots, he had asked for an Ethiopian model. As a side-effect of working with an Ethiopian software development team over the last few years, and

— • 197 • —

thus visiting Addis Ababa a number of times, he had become increasingly impressed with the beauty of Ethiopian woman. A beautiful young black female robot, outspoken, intelligent, curious, ambitious... she had just seemed right for so many reasons. But he had not yet worked with her much; she was still new. While Sonny looked insanely curious and sometimes just insane, Aden looked like the next President of the World. She just needed to be woken up.

And in the dream he had just had... whoa... no... She had not been President of the World. She had been wrapped up in the mess of real life. Still, she had been so beautifully alive, so vibrant, so mental, physical and emotional...

So in love with Sonny...

A memory of Sonny's exploding head and various hallucinogenic dolphins wafted through his memory. He shook his head back and forth, fast.

Whoa.

The dream was gone; the robots were there; the whole three of them, quite beautiful, and still inanimate for the moment.

And one robot was missing, right? Who was it? Ah – Ana – the star of the show – the beautiful young female robot ... classical European with a light touch of Asian – Where was Ana? She was usually off giving demos somewhere or other, to potential investors or partners, or up on the podium in front of a conference.

Ana had more motors in her face than any of the others, enabling more precisely contoured expressions, and she was generally everyone's favorite – except his. He didn't dislike her exactly, but she didn't tug his heart like Sonny, or Aden, or Phil. Perhaps she was too mainstream for his eccentric imagination.

So was that why -- ?

An image of the robot judge from his dream popped up, suddenly more vivid than the room in front of him. That had been Ana's face. Ana's. What was it about beautiful white women passing judgment on him, he wondered? – something that troubled his psyche? Did Ana look like he remembered his mother looking, half a century ago when he'd stared up at her from the crib? A bit, maybe.... But his mother had never passed judgment like that – she had always been a kind woman – and she still was a kind woman, in strikingly good health and acute mind as she worked her way through her early 70s –

Anyway, there the Ana judge was, passing sentence on humanity. Was humanity guilty of inhumanity to itself? Of course it was. But wasn't this part of the secret to its growth?

All those weird scenes had just been a creation of his psyche, Gen Burtzle realized – the robot judge, the love affair of Aden and Sonny, the Phil Dick robot's impassioned defense of the race that had created him.

The reality was, these robots could pass only the simplest of judgments, at the moment. They had trouble judging whether they were talking to a potential investor or a high school student, unless things were spelled out to them very clearly. They were still at the research stage. Research he played a key role in.

Gradually, the reality of the situation sank in.

His friend and colleague, Hans Davidson, interrupted his thoughts, noting his dazed state and asking "Late night last night?"

There he was – Hans – and unlike the robots, he was alive here, just like in the dream. Full of energy and charisma and ideas as always.

"Yeah, I was up at the computer until 3." Gen yawned widely. "Whoa, I totally drifted off there."

"Yes you did," Hans laughed.

"Man, I had some fucking weird dreams," said Gen slowly, still just half-awake.

"Do tell!" Hans exclaimed.

"About these robots... the three of them.... But they weren't all robots. Aden was a human. And there was some kind of court case. Phil Dick was defending humanity."

"He liked to do that," Hans nodded.

Gen drank some water from a glass, gulping it down his throat, with the aim of waking himself up. "Yeah, I guess so."

"The dream had a lot of parts," Gen recollected, staring blankly at the three robots. "I can't put it all into words right now... my head's still halfway there..."

Davidson raised his eyebrows, "Did you make mischief with the nine-dimensional machine-elves again?"

"Essentially…" Gen said slowly… finally adding, "Words are an awkward medium for evoking certain sorts of patterns."

"Ah…," said Hans enthusiastically, "But even a vision you cannot describe in words can still inspire what you do! I can't put into words most of the visions that inspire me. I mean… I have written some things, but I always run into limits. So, instead of trying to write all my visions down, I'm here making robots!"

"You can describe your vision in robots."

"And then, infused with the wisdom of your AGI software, the robots can get smart enough to describe their own visions!"

"A vision that envisions itself… and re-visions itself…!" Gen exclaimed.

Hans pumped his fist in the air in triumph, "Yes!"

"That weird dream is still bouncing around in my head, man."

"Do you want to try some trepanation, to make a hole for it to escape? We do have a drill in the other room."

"Thanks for the generous offer." Gen took a deep breath, musingly.

"Sometimes," Hans recalled, "a dream feels more than a dream; you know what I mean? Like it really is a trip to another universe… or at least another part of this universe…

like you've been teleported out into the system-containing metacosm – for just a bit."

"Maybe you did!" Gen grinned, his friend's enthusiasm boosting him.

"And teleporting out of this spacetime for a bit, of course, it's like you're escaping for an eternity. I mean, this whole space and time axis are just part of a little corner of the metacosm. There's a whole lot of pattern space out there." Han nodded, agreeing with himself. Agreeing with the universe!

"You know," said Gen, "the main thing I always take from experiences like that... that dream or whatever... is just how damn ignorant I am. I mean... we all are; not just me in particular."

"Yes!" Hans affirmed enthusiastically.

"It's like I always say when I'm giving a speech on the future – we, humans, trying to predict what comes next after the advent of superhuman AI, is like a cockroach trying to predict who will win World War III – or which startup company will obsolete Face book ... we just don't have the basis..."

Irina Vanyavich, another friend and colleague, looked up from her desk on the other side of the room and interrupted, "But we do have some things cockroaches don't, right? Like general intelligence and compassion... At least now and then..."

"Yeah, we do. But, I mean... whatever comes next after us, it will also have its own new traits that we don't have –

things we totally can't understand any better than cockroaches understand general intelligence and compassion."

Hans probed, "Or is compassion a basic principle of the universe? That seems to be the message Phil Dick was giving us…"

Gen interrupted… "One of the messages…"

"Yeah…"

Gen added, seated back in his chair, "My friend, Spyder, at the Global Brain Institute… he likes to talk about 'open-ended intelligence.' I think there's some wisdom there. That's really the crux of it."

"I mean… yeah… that's what evolution is…"

"But evolution can be harsh."

"But compassion is evolving too," Hans pointed out. "Evolution is evolving itself."

"Evolution of evolution of evolution of evolution… *Evolulution?*"

"*Evolulululululution!*" Hans exclaimed, laughing. The two laughed together now.

"You people are silly," observed Irina.

"We evolved that way," Gen protested…. "We evolvolvolvolvolvolved that way…"

Smiling, Irina asked him sarcastically, "Are you stoned or what?"

"More than stoned, I think...," Gen snickered.

Hans added, more seriously, "Intelligence is evolution, and evolution is intelligence. And the evolution of compassion is a big part of the whole dynamic."

"Let's hope so."

"So far...I mean... the rise of robots and AI scares some people. I guess because people are wired to fear the unknown... yet so far, really, robots and AI are doing way more good than harm... We have elder care robots; AIs discovering new drugs to extend life; AI scientists, engineers, artists, AI's composing music to bring people joy and expand their lives!" he gestures in the air, his eyes animatedly stares at Ben.

Nodding, Gen responded, "Well, yeah. And robots doing all the mechanical work people find tedious; transforming energy into various forms so we can eat and breathe and fly and so on. It's like I always say... robots eliminating human jobs is a feature not a bug. And people merging with robots to become superhuman minds – superhuman in ethics and judgment as well as intelligence – certainly this will involve some loss, but also so much gain, right? Whether we call it the emergence of a new kind of human or a new kind of robot..."

"Well, people are already known to be fucked up," said Hans, his tone semi-serious. "The jury's still out regarding robots."

"Everything is fucked up in its own unique way."

"Evolution of evolution of evolution of evolulululululution of fucked-uppedness...!"

"And compassion!" Gen added.

"Yes!"

An Ethiopian engineer, Natnael, walked into the room and stood in front of the Sonny robot. He stared at it for a moment and asked Gen and David, "How's he doing?"

"All right, I think," Hans answered. "The face animations are in pretty good shape."

"The deep learning vision stuff we put in the Atom space is actually working all right," added Gen. "We can recognize boundaries of a lot of events now. Like this conversation... he can tell it was a new event when you came in to talk to me; and that this event will end when you leave...unless I leave with you."

"That's the information theory stuff we were talking about yesterday, right?" Irina asked.

"Yeah; the principle is that an event boundary is a discontinuity of predictability," Gen explains, getting enmeshed in reality again, but half his brain still stuck in that long amazing dream... "The subtlety is in how you measure predictability. You have to measure it based on all your prior knowledge of the world... and you need to do that quickly, each moment, in the middle of your perception algorithm."

"How about the reasoning system...?" Natnael asked.

Gen asked as he moved towards Natnael, "You mean, does he actually understand what's going on at all? Noel has been working on it. It's better than last week, sure. You can ask him some questions."

Natnael then turns to Sonny, "How are you doing, Sonny boy?"

The Sonny robot responded, "I am doing *ok*, Natnael. How are you?"

"Pretty good... pretty good. I had a bit of a cold this weekend, but I'm starting to feel better now."

"I'm sorry to hear you had a cold this weekend. I'm glad to hear you're starting to feel better now."

Turning to Gen now, Natnael said, "Yeah, not bad. The surface realization is still a bit wonky, though."

Gen looked Sonny straight in the eyes, trying to see something there. A tear rolled down his cheek, surprising him. His arm shifted instinctively, with the intention to wipe it off, but his cognition intervened. Let the tear flow – why not? The missing intelligence – the mindfulness the robot had had in his dream; the mindfulness he knew it would have in the future or some similar robot would have; the limited diffusion of intelligence and wisdom throughout time and space; it all just seemed so sad sometimes. It all deserved a tear, or a trillion. If his colleagues noticed him crying over nothing, so what? Why was human culture so constricted? And why, why, why did inanimate objects have to be so stupid? Or were they, really? Was there intelligence ambient in everything, and he was just too stupid – too wrapped up in his stupid human culture -- to grok the preponderance of it? But then, why did he and his goddamned culture have to be too stupid to grok it? Why did the universal mind prefer to make parts of itself so retarded? He wanted to cry out a river of tears, broad enough and wild enough to swallow up the multiverse. But what would be the point of trying…. His tears would end up numbering only in the thousands, or the tens of thousands at most, before his eyes dried up and got insanely sore – his vain, pointless, localized effort at swallowing up the cosmos with sad water would not make the world any more intelligent or any more compassionate.

Gen thought of the engineers in the office around him, working concentratedly and industriously. Why, he asked himself, do you have to think so much, and feel so much? Why not just do stuff, like they do?

But sometimes you do do that, he reminded himself. You're a techie too. You do a lot. You're just in a weird mood.

And the real question is – why do you have to think so LITTLE, and feel so LITTLE? What the heck is with this miniscule, petty, partitioned-off human existence? The robot judge was right, no?

Of course you think she was right; she was just a split-off portion of your psyche.

Or was she?

Realizing he had paused an oddly long time in the midst of a relatively straightforward conversation, Gen pointed at Sonny to refocus his own attention. He said to Natnael, "I mean… it's *all* a bit wonky still; but we're getting there."

Hans answered, "Yes, we are."

Gen looked at Natnael and said, "About the surface realization... that's mostly a matter of attention allocation. I mean, the right phrasings are in there in the Atom space... or at least, they are implicit in the Atom space after a few inference steps. They just aren't being selected. The problem is that the parameters of the ECAN dynamics are still fixed." He leaned forward. "We've always known we need to make them adaptive, we just haven't done it yet."

"Who's working on that? Can we have it working in time for the Future Forum?" Hans asked urgently.

"Two weeks from now? Fuck...," Gen said, pausing to mentally enumerate the various aspects of the task.

Natnael thought for a moment. "Yeah, well... maybe... Probably, I guess..."

"I'm still halfway in dream-land, though." said Gen. "I'm gonna go walk around outside a few minutes and try to regain my consciousness!"

"Alright...!" Hans waved at him. "I'm gonna get some work done on these faces."

Gen left the building where the Davidson Robotics office was and walked through the Science Park campus, heading for the waterfront. Occasionally, someone walked by; but mostly, he had the area to himself.

For the last few years he hadn't remembered many of his dreams. But whoa, what an exception! The long dream from his long nap on the chair kept pouring into his mind, like an unearthly fluid from a transdimensional firehose.

A few times during his life he had regularly lucid-dreamed. But the dreams he'd controlled himself hadn't had the same archetypal power of his deepest involuntary dreams – like this last one.

Robots that could walk and talk and think like humans – and more – like the ones in the dream he'd just had -- this was indeed the goal of his team's work at Davidson Robotics. From the perspective of his long-term goals as an Artificial General Intelligence researcher, the creation of human-like robots was just a relatively simple intermediate goal – the real goal was massively superintelligent, superbenevolent, supercreative engineered minds. Well, such minds would be largely self-engineered in the end; all he and his colleagues could hope to do was provide a decent initial condition. Teach them to build themselves, give them a positive philosophy of themselves and humanity and world, and let them go – let the next step of evolution in humanity's corner of the cosmos take its course –

But it was easy to lose track of the grand long-term goals in the mess of the nitty-gritty, day-by-day work. One of his main roles at Davidson was precisely to keep the tech team focused on the big picture while they ground through the highly difficult, often tedious work of designing, developing and debugging software and hardware for thinking machines. And even for him, the Grand Visionary, sometimes it was hard to keep track of the grand vision and not to get frustrated by the sheer amount and complexity of the labor required to make the vision real. Especially when the company funding the work was repeatedly on the verge of running out of cash – always saved at the last minute, so far, by Hans Davidson's brilliance and charisma, which could be judiciously translated into fundraising prowess when the situation required it desperately enough; and by the growing enthusiasm of investors for snazzy robots and clever software.

Would it be possible to create intelligent, autonomous robots like the ones in his long, weird dream? Of course it would. Of this Gen rarely had any real doubt. Consciousness was mysterious in some regards, but the self-organizing physical systems that advanced reflective consciousness attached itself to – these were not so mysterious, just complex and complicated on multiple levels. From paramecium to worm to bug to fish to lizard to rat to ape to human – to autonomous human-level robo-intelligence and then beyond, far beyond – it was all just self-organizing pattern systems, arranged hierarchically and heterarchically. Minds were systems for recognizing patterns in themselves and the world – including patterns regarding what processes tended to help them achieve their goals in what contexts ... including goals related to self-modification and self-improvement...

Would he and Hans and their team be the ones to make the breakthrough to machine superintelligence? That, Gen wavered on now and then.

That they understood the problem better than anyone else on the planet, he had little doubt. He had written out a plan for engineering human-level intelligence, with a couple of his AI colleagues. It was the only moderately detailed blueprint for a mind on the planet, so far as he knew! It explained how all the different aspects of human-like memory and thinking fit together. Facts and beliefs and observations and procedures and senses and actions, all stored in the same representation.   Logical reasoning, nonlinear spreading of attention, evolution-like creative learning, imaginative concept-blending – all working together, integrated tightly to allow them to help each other out in cases of difficulty.   All embedded in a framework enabling an agent – like a robot – to figure out what procedures would help it best achieve its goals in its currently perceived and understood context.   Yeah, imperfect as it surely was, Gen Burtzle was proud of his Design for a Thinking Machine.

But still -- there were better-funded groups around, who were no dummies either. Gen had intentionally eschewed taking a job with a big tech company, because he didn't like the culture and he wanted to be sure everything he did would remain open source and freely sharable with everyone on the planet. He had allied himself with Hans instead – which was a heck of a lot of fun, and worked out well in that Hans was also psyched about open-source software (though much of the hardware underlying his robots was proprietary).   But Davidson Robotics couldn't supply the staff, data or compute power of a Google, IBM or Baidu.   What it did have was wild, crazy, chaotic imagination and energy.   Which, he felt deep down, was worth more than money.   But more money would have been good too....   With the inspiration and understanding of him and Hans and their team, and the funds of a big tech company, might they have already brought Sonny as alive as he'd been in that dream – that DREAM –

Had that really been just a dream? It had seemed like more.

But what then? A glimpse of the future? A peek into some alternate reality? An error in the multiverse? A bug in the software implementing the simulation he'd become habituated to call reality – in the Matrix?

Ten years ago he had given a talk at a futurist conference, titled "How to Launch a Positive Singularity in at Most Ten Years." The first step in the ten year plan had been for someone with a lot of money to donate at least ten million dollars to the endeavor, to get the first batch of the work done. With ten million dollars, he had reckoned, enough of his design for AI could be implemented to yield an AI system with amazing demonstrable behaviors (such as an AI biologist making major medical discoveries ... or, though he hadn't known Hans at the time, a humanoid robot carrying out intelligent commonsense conversations...).

After that point, after there were sufficiently amazing demonstrable behaviors, raising further funding would be no problem. And with massive funding, his full design for superintelligence could be implemented rapidly and correctly on the world's best hardware, with all the little gaps filled in by the world's best scientists. Why not? Didn't the creation of the next intelligent species deserve as much material and cognitive and social resources as, say, the search for a cure for cancer, or the manufacture of faster semiconductor chips, or the concoction of new exotic derivatives for financial traders to use, or the design and manufacture and distribution of luxury handbags?

But the ten million hadn't come, though he'd gotten enough bits and pieces of funding from various sources – most recently from Davidson Robotics – to keep his AI project going in a meaningful way.   The ten million hadn't come, and ten years had passed, and there was still no Singularity. Perhaps if he'd been born rich he would have been able to do it by now – to create a Singularity with the wealth he'd inherited, by putting it toward implementation of his AI designs. But then, perhaps if he'd born rich, he wouldn't have had the kind of childhood consistent with creating a workable AI design, which wasn't an especially easy thing to do.

Or perhaps if he'd been more handsome, and more ruthless, and managed to seduce a wealthy heiress – instead of marrying for love, as he'd done over and over again, with mixed results.   His new marriage was going rather well, fingers crossed … he felt a pang of longing for his wife Lingling, who was away speaking at a conference for a few days, on her own research in computational chemistry. He wondered for a moment why, in his dream last night, Sonny and Aden had never really consummated their love – or had they, and he'd just forgotten it?

Like Lingling and himself, Sonny and Aden had come from different cultures – well, more so, different species. But he and his wife had opened themselves up to each other, and had come to love each other fully, transcending their individual boundaries and coming together to explore new realms of ecstatic experience – well at least on a good day.   There were some fucking shitty days too, but he preferred not to preoccupy with them. As Aden had said in the dream – love exists to overcome separation.   Or something like that.   Sonny and Aden hadn't got there. Yet. Maybe they would have, if his head hadn't blown up.

What would it feel like to have your head blow up while fucking?

Maybe like nothing, if it happened to fast for you to feel it.

But what if you were a robot? You could feel things much faster then.

Or what if he had just been a better salesman – plenty of other people had raised tens of millions of dollars for their tech projects. He had just failed due to being a better AI designer than fundraiser.   Fortunately Hans was good at fundraising … but he was raising funds for his robotics hardware and aesthetics work, and then for Gen's AI work on the side … it was a lot even for a superhero like Hans Davidson.

In any case, he reminded himself, it really didn't matter if it was his own team that achieved superhuman AI first. If he were hit by a truck, or his head exploded during sex, someone else would create thinking machines and the next generation of intelligent species would get built anyway. And would open doors to new dimensions of experience, perhaps contacting and resonating with uber-intelligences already existing all around, in the vibrations of all the elementary particles --

Gen laughed at himself as he strolled. This sort of rambling, counterfactual thinking was pointless, he knew. He usually didn't indulge himself in it – well at least not for this long, not in the middle of the day like this.   Well, it wasn't the middle of the day – it was almost the evening. But he tended to work all day and then all evening, so it was the middle of his workday, right?

Work, work, work. And he and his team were making steady, sometimes exciting progress on their work, due to their endless work – even though the really generally intelligent machines and the superhuman superintelligences still lived in the realm of --

The sky grew suddenly darker, as he walked across the campus. The shift in luminance paused his meandering, and he stopped for a moment and simply admired the dusky beauty of the place. He strode to the railing that lined the Science Park waterfront, gazing out over the bay, taking in the light on the water and the small waves, and the far-off trees and buildings on the other side. A song he'd been listening to the previous day, "The Final Truth" by Lunatic Soul, echoed lightly in his head.

And he sank into reverie again – inevitably. That's why he had walked outside, after all, to stare at the dreamy water and the misty air, and feel them resonate with the misty dreams and dreamy mist of his – what was it? thinking? wondering? hoping? dreaming? speculating? tripping out on weird plots and visions? Whatever…

One by one, ghostly, not-quite-substantial forms, comprising several human individuals, appeared near him. They were also standing by the railing facing the bay and looking out. Hans Davidson; Sonny Davidson the robot; Philip K. Dick – was it the robot or the real man, or something else entirely? … Mary Rose, the insecure, sexually frustrated psycho-bitch; Bob Dobbs … or was that a chimpanzee? ... Aden... Aden, Aden. He was a little bit in love with that robot, he realized for the umpteenth time... He had been even before that long dream.

At first they all looked human; then it became clear that only their bodies and faces were human, the backs of their heads being all robotic. The wires in their heads were clearly visible. The glowing, flickering lights within, flashing out through their plastic back-skulls.

After Gen stood there for a while, co-existing with the phantasms, an elderly Chinese woman with long white hair and a walking stick walked past. She came and stood next to him, quietly and peacefully, looking out at the clouds.

She looked over at Gen and spoke, "Seen a ghost, have you?"

Gen looked at her meaningfully and paused before speaking. "In a way..."

"There are a lot of them around."

"Around this river, you mean?" he asked, gesturing toward the water.

The old woman nodded with a slight smile. Gen looked out at the river again.

"Tell me."

Gen stared the old woman in the eye, intently. "I work with a company here called Davidson Robotics. We work on making robots that look and act just like people. My part of it is mostly the AI. I work on trying to make the robots think like people... and ultimately much better than people. I mean, humans are not possibly the most intelligent of minds, nor are they the most loving and compassionate. There are all sorts of possible minds we can create."

The old woman nodded. The two of them looked out across the water to the mountains beyond.

"Of course we're not quite there yet," he clarified. "There's still a lot of research to do. But... anyway... yeah... I fell asleep in the lab today and I sort of..."

Gen paused a long while. The old woman thought a bit.

"You had a dream," she said; and he nodded.

"A long and meaningful one...," she continued.

"So it seemed."

She stared at him brazenly, her brown eyes wide and welcoming.

"It's too much to tell it all," he said. "But... well... it was a future world where we had succeeded; where our robots were really alive and where they could think like people... and in some ways even better. "

"And were the robots friendly – in your dream?" she asked.

"Some of them were friendly, loving and curious, yeah. And others... well, kind of, the opposite. There was one robot – she's one of our research robots in the lab. A beautiful woman robot... But in my dream, she was kind of a judge, seated in some, sort of, courtroom."

The woman asked, intrigued, "Judging you?"

Gen smiled, "And you! Judging all of humanity..."

The woman nodded at Gen and looked him over slowly, then looked at the river. "When I was a child, I used to wonder what an alien species would think if it came to earth and looked around. All the wars, the cruelty and suffering... Rich men accumulating wealth in their palaces and mansions while the poor huddle outside their walls, starving and laden with disease. Parents hurting their children and husbands and wives making each other's lives miserable, day after day..."

Gen nodded, listening raptly... She stared back at him, and continued, "People working in mind-numbing or back-breaking labor, hour after hour, month after month, year after year; just to accumulate enough money to buy food for their families...or worse yet, to buy unnecessary luxury goods, serving only as status symbols. The aliens would land, I thought, take a careful look around, and then get back in their spaceships and go back home." She shrugged.

Nodding at her, Gen crossed his arms. He smiled. "And what do you think now?"

"I ... think a lot less than I used to. This world is a complicated place, full of layers and tangles and mysteries; and as you say, the human mind isn't all that smart. I find myself less and less convinced that any of us, me very much included, really understands what's going on here; who we are; what we are; or even why we're here. And I find myself less and less worried about it. This world has so much suffering and horror... and also so much beauty and wonder and love. More and more I find myself preoccupied with the beauty. The twist of the plant stem; the loving gaze between two friends walking together talking... The movement of the water and the boats that people ride on it..." She suddenly gestured toward the view. "Look!"

She waved toward the water and the clouds. A ferry went past in the distance. A young couple was laughing somewhere behind them, chatting in Cantonese. Human absurdity, human love...

Gen looked around and out across the water, taking in the landscape; trying not to look just at the ghost-faces, which had now migrated into the clouds. He nodded again, "Fair enough. But then, what about your aliens...? Do you still think they'd go back home?"

"I think... I think they'd look at us... all of us, doing all that we do, the great and the terrible and the mundane and everyday... the boring and the fascinating stuff... the amazing work you do building robots; and the tables of numbers accumulated by the accountants in the high-rises of the Hong Kong island ... and the dissidents tortured in prisons ... and the birds and the clouds and the forests..."

Gen got distracted from the woman for a moment, as a kid about two years old ran past them, his mother hurriedly – but with reasonably good humor -- following the tot a few feet behind.

The old woman's eyes followed the kid also, and she added, "And children enjoying their bodies, and the sex and the love that gives rise to them." She paused for a moment, thinking... "And children dying of malnutrition just an eight-hour flight away in Africa... I think they would look at all this and be amazed at the unique beauty and the beautiful uniqueness of it all."

"So," asked Gen, trying to be sure he understood, "they'd look at our world like, a Hieronymus Bosch painting from an alien solar system, or something. A bit twisted and ugly in places, but wonderfully beautiful overall...?"

"Yes, I think so." The old woman pondered for a moment and nodded, "Something like that. If they were advanced enough to build a spaceship to come here from so far away, they would be advanced enough to appreciate the beauty in every corner of the universe. They would see the beauty in human dreams, in human faith, in human life and love. Along with all the mess, of course..."

Gen took a deep breath and asked, "And you think the same about the robot judge in my dream? If a robot were smart enough to judge us in any kind of seriousness, it would be smart enough to appreciate the beauty in our humanity; the beauty and love that shine through all the chaos and mess and stupidity and the madness and the pain..."

"Yes."

"It's a beautiful idea."

The two of them stood there for a few moments, looking out at the clouds and the water in silence. A large gust of wind came up, blowing both of their hair around wildly; then subsided a bit. The old woman exhaled. She smiled at Gen. "I should be going. I'll see you around."

Grateful, Gen responded, "See you. Thanks for the words of wisdom."

"Words of wisdom," he mused. It's so rare to utter that phrase non-sarcastically.

She grinned warmly and walked off, in the opposite direction from which she had come. But after she got a few feet away, she turned around and said, "If you want to talk some more sometime, come see me. I sit and draw quite often, behind the Vietnamese restaurant on Lamma Island. I can tell you about the Mindplex, if you like. If I'm not there drawing, the folks who run the restaurant know me well...."

"The Mindplex...?" Gen asked.

"I'm tired now," said the woman, smiling warmly. "Another time..."

Gen stood there, staring at the face-ghosts in the clouds, which were more intense than ever. Aden, Han, Phil Dick, the stony-faced robot judge... They looked so alive, so real.

He ran after the woman, impulsively. "Wait a moment," he said, when he caught up to her, putting his hand on her shoulder lightly.

She turned to face him, silently.

"That wasn't just a dream, was it?" he said.

She just kept staring...

"Mindplex..." he said, quietly, waiting for the word to trigger something in her or in him.

"You saw a ball in the dream, right?" she asked, in a measured voice. "A transparent ball of sorts – a big one –"

"Aden did," he answered quickly, the image popping up in his mind with unsettling vividity. "A ball floating in an ocean – an ocean of peoples' thoughts. A ball full of peoples' thoughts, floating on an ocean of peoples' thoughts…. Like it was a tool for focusing something – focusing the collective mind maybe – but not just that –"

She nodded.

"Does that ball mean something particular?" he asked. "It didn't seem particularly important in the context of everything else that was going on."

"We'll discuss that later," she said vaguely, in a tone that broached no further inquisition.

"It wasn't just a dream," he repeated.

She just looked … and he continued hastily: "Ah, but then it's all just a dream, right?"

She grinned a bit, shifting her body as if she was about to resume walking.

"But even if everything is a dream, some dreams are more everything than others," he laughed. "Or something like that…."

"Something," she concurred, with a soft and wise smile.

"Others have had dreams like this too," he guessed. "There's some specific cause to it."

"Causation – " she began.

"Yes, I know, that's the wrong concept," he interrupted – remembering the robot judge's attitude toward causation, in his dream. Yes, it was a fraught concept. He'd actually done some work on the mathematical foundations of causation. He could talk about that for hours or days -- "But that's not the point right now…. I'm just thinking – all of are tied up in knots, you know? It's part of being human."

She nodded.

"Our bodies get tied up in knots, and yoga tries to undo them. Our minds get tied up in knots, and we try to release them with meditation and psychedelics and so forth."

"Meditation or medication," she laughed, slightly.

"Exactly! That's what the judge in my dream was talking about. But her view was that untying the knots basically isn't worthwhile – because I guess if you untie the knots there's nothing left…. Nothing of humanity, I mean…."

A thought popped into his head, and he chuckled. "It's like when your shoelaces get in a really big knot. If the knot's bad but not too bad, you spend time on untying it. But after a certain point, if the knot's too screwed up, you just give up and throw the shoelace out – it costs less to buy a new one than the time you'd spend untying the old one would be worth, right?

"But then that depends on how rich you are. If you're poor enough you could spend four hours untying that shoelace…..

"And then there's the process – untying the lace has a certain satisfaction to it, right?   Though so does throwing out the fucked-up lace – it has the satisfaction that you don't have to struggle with the damn fucking knot anymore…

"But the point is, the process of untying the knots of the human mind and body has a certain beauty to it, right?   Or at least it feels that way sometimes….

"But that's just 'the purpose of love is to overcome separation / the purpose of separation is to give an opportunity for love' again, hmmm…. Does it always come back to that?

"Hah, I'm just wasting your time with philosophical bullshit," he said, noting a certain look in her face, not quite sure if it was impatience.   "Sorry, I'm in a weird mood tonight."

"Don't apologize," she said. "It's not bullshit…."

He laughed.   "At least no more than the rest of this?" He waved his arms, gesturing at her, himself, the water, the sky, their world.

"Exactly!" she agreed, taking a breath. "But I do have to go," she said, warmly.   "But really -- do come look me up sometime.   I mean, give it a few days at least.   Let this recent dream you've had – whatever it may mean – settle in your mind. And then –"

Gen closed his eyes, took a deep breath, and nodded. When he opened his eyes, the old woman was gone. Not just walked a few meters away – gone! He looked around and there was nowhere to be seen, and also nowhere she could have gotten to that rapidly, without running at trans-Olympic speed.

How did she walk off so quickly? Was she a ghost as well? What was the point of "mindplex"? So strange…… But then a lot was so strange lately….

He looked back at the clouds as the ghost-faces gradually faded away. Soon, there were only clouds again; barely a trace of face. Furthermore, the clouds were somewhat parting, and some sunny blue sky was emerging. He looked up at the azure expanse, watched a bird fly past, then bent his head down looking at the water just below. He made a slight, ambiguous smile; and closed his eyes, sinking into something between thought and memory.

Acknowledgements

The core themes of this book emerged in my mind, in large part, as a consequence of my work over the last few years with David Hanson and his company Hanson Robotics.

Obviously, the weird ideas pursued here have no direct connection with the practical commercial work Hanson Robotics does ... and nor are they the same as the weird ideas in David's head as he creates, works with, and dreams about his robot characters.

But still, to a large extent, David's vision of humanlike – but not quite human – robot characters, as amazing artifacts in themselves and as steps on the path to a compassionate Singularity, is what stimulated my imagination to produce this here tale.

And since David and I were both independently inspired by Phil Dick and his obsessions with simulation and compassion and human nature, it is only too appropriate that David's Phil Dick robot plays a critical role in the story.

This book also owes its existence to my wonderful wife Ruiting Lian – not only for her overall love and inspiration, which helps me form a mental space in which to create ... but also for her determined last-minute work on her PhD thesis in early 2016. For a while there she was pulling 18+ hour days aiming to get her thesis done by a certain deadline imposed by her university (Xiamen University); and on a certain 3 day weekend, I decided to sit next to her in our shared study at our apartment in Yuen Leng Tsuen, in the New Territories of Hong Kong, and match her crazy work hours. Initially I was going to spend the weekend doing technical stuff, but then I got possessed with the notion of writing a screenplay based on the robots we were working with at Hanson Robotics…

The somewhat crude screenplay I wrote during that 3 day weekend of minimal sleep, was afterwards – at a far more gradual pace – transformed into this novel.

Ruiting also inspired a series of poems that I wrote in early 2016, some passages from which were cribbed to serve as the seed for Sonny's delirious poetico-ramblings in the middle of Aden's hallucination. The acute reader will note some allusions to Octavio Paz in there as well.

The general idea of writing a screenplay tracking a human-robot love story had popped up a few months earlier in a conversation with my father, Ted Goertzel.   The original idea was to make it something like a conventional talky romantic comedy – but with a one of the characters a robot. But in the midst of writing, as usually happens with me, things got changed around a bit. I still remember the moment of delight when the scene with the exploding sex robot occurred to me, and the greater moment of delight when the scene with the judge occurred!

Thanks are also due to Mari Sabino and Leira Micah Gianni Roman for their edits and advice, largely but not wholly regarding the first part of the book (the Aden-Sonny romance). Mari worked with me on the original screenplay version, and Leira helped with the conversion from screenplay to novel. Each lent their own combination of literary skill and human perspective. And thanks are due to Mercy Njari for proofreading and syntax edits.

The art on the front cover was concocted by a rank amateur digital artist named Dr. Ben Goertzel. The cover design is the work of the inimitable Zarko Paunovic.

45145531R00131

Made in the USA
San Bernardino, CA
01 February 2017